## Praise for James Sallis's Books

"Sallis might be one of the best writers in America . . . If you're not acquainted with his work, this is a fine place to start."

—***The Cleveland Plain Dealer* on *Cypress Grove***

"Sallis writes lean, sinewy prose that grabs your attention from the start and holds it fast to the end . . . Smooth as aged bourbon."

—***The Philadelphia Inquirer* on *Cripple Creek***

"Brilliant and poignant . . . Sallis has a poet's eye and ear, and his compact prose is redolent with the music (literal and otherwise) of rural Tennesse." —***The Seattle Times* on *Cripple Creek***

"A fierce and original writer working at full power."

—***Los Angeles Times* on *Ghost of a Flea***

"James Sallis may be the 'purest' writer of crime fiction in America today . . . his books are worth reading solely for what rises from the inspired use of language."

—***San Francisco Chronicle* on *Salt River***

"Extraordinary . . . Justly compared to James Lee Burke and Raymond Chandler."

—***Los Angeles Times* on *The Long-Legged Fly***

"Sallis is a poet in private eye's clothing."

—***The Boston Globe***

"[Sallis] brings to his thriller a lyrical style not often found in the genre." —***The San Diego Union-Tribune* on *Salt River***

"James Sallis breathes new life into the wheezing detective genre."

***—The San Francisco Chronicle***

"Sallis is a rare find . . . A fine prose stylist with an interest in moral struggle and a gift for the lacerating evocation of loss."

***—Long Island Newsday***

"A taut page-turner . . . It's a lovely piece of work that makes you wish some other writers would take lessons from him."

***—The Washington Post* on *Drive***

"Sallis's allusive, haunting prose sometimes has the surreal quality of Anais Nin's novels, and *Bluebottle* offers dark truths about racism and the search for identity."

***—Detroit Free Press* on *Bluebottle***

"Spare but eloquent . . . [A] superior series."

***—The New York Times Book Review* on**
***Cripple Creek* and the Turner trilogy**

"In addition to his masterly novels, Sallis is known for his work as a poet, and the lyrical beauty of his words shines through his pages . . . It's a crime that a writer this good isn't better known."

***—Chicago Sun-Times* on *Cripple Creek***

"Sallis' lyricism and power trump everything else."

***—The Cleveland Plain Dealer* on *Cripple Creek***

# THE KILLER IS DYING

A Novel

JAMES SALLIS

WALKER & COMPANY
NEW YORK

For information address Walker & Company, 175 Fifth Avenue, New York, New York 10010.

Published by Walker Publishing Company, Inc., New York

All papers used by Walker & Company are natural, recyclable products made from wood grown in well-managed forests. The manufacturing processes conform to the environmental regulations of the country of origin.

LIBRARY OF CONGRESS CATALOGING-IN-PUBLICATION DATA

Sallis, James, 1944–
The killer is dying / by James Sallis. —1st U.S. ed.
p. cm.
ISBN 978-0-8027-7945-8 (hardcover)
1. Phoenix (Ariz.)—Fiction. I. Title.
PS3569.A462K55 2011
813'.54—dc22
2010038548

Visit Walker & Company's website at www.walkerbooks.com

First U.S. edition published by Walker & Company in 2011
This paperback edition published in 2012

Paperback ISBN: 978-0-8027-7947-2

1 3 5 7 9 10 8 6 4 2

Typeset by Westchester Book Group
Printed in the U.S.A. by Quad/Graphics, Fairfield, Pennsylvania

*To Karyn,*
*for just about everything*

# CHAPTER ONE

HE IS AWAKE AGAIN, with no idea what time it may be, or whether, really, he has slept at all. He sleeps poorly these days. Strange, too, how time's become a blur. At first there's no reason to know the time of day, then days themselves give way, finally years. Till only the change of seasons marks another passage, another decline. To remember, he has to think back to where he lived, what rented room or cheap apartment in Gary, Gretna, Memphis, Seattle.

There are no streetlights in this part of the city. These are reserved for kinder, gentler regions to the north and east. Here, it is about as dark as dark gets. Light from the billboard across the street, its legend in Spanish and advertising the latest luxury vehicle, enters the room at a slant. It does little more, he thinks, than blur the darkness.

Periodically he lifts one hand, the left, into that light, closes his fingers to a fist and opens them again, watching the play of muscle, tendons, and scars. As the hand opens, it begins to shake. That's the drugs. The drugs make him shake. But without the drugs he shakes more. The drugs make him stupid, too—and he can't afford to be stupid.

He hears two people shouting at one another outside, on the balcony the next floor up, from the sound of it.

"It's my fucking money!"

"And it's *my* fucking car!"

Then the rimshot of someone getting slammed against a wall or door.

A radio or TV in the next room drones on as it has for the four days he has been here. It's tuned to talk shows, words indistinguishable, only the cadence and inflection changing with hosts, callers or guests, commercial announcements. From time to time another voice, that of the room's occupant, joins in, as though in conversation.

He gets up and, feet swollen, pads to the bathroom. A cockroach that had been drinking from the bowl flows up the side of the sink and vanishes over the edge when the light goes on. With a razorblade he splits one of the pills in half. They stop the shaking, for a time. An hour, two. And while they don't help the pain, they do cause the world to go soft in interesting ways. Walls curve outward, corners and angles retreat, everything slows. As though transparent panes have gone up between himself and all else.

While there he fills and drinks from the glass that, hating the smell and taste of plastic, he carries with him from place to place. The pills leave him permanently cotton-mouthed.

In T-shirt and boxers, he steps out onto the walkway. The clamor from the balcony above has subsided. He realizes that he had almost forgotten where he is, but now the far-off lights, low buildings, and sprawl of dark sky remind him. Out on the street, past the cracked black asphalt of a parking lot that looks like lava flow, a lowrider cruises by at fifteen miles an hour. It's a Ford

Galaxie from the fifties, tricked out with spinners for caps and painted all over with bright-colored dragons and iridescent, half-naked women. In the distance he hears what have to be gunshots from a large-bore handgun. The shots are clean, distinct, clearly separated. From that direction, within moments, a siren cries, then abruptly cuts off.

There is another sound, though. In the eaves of this low-end, by-the-week motel, in an angled joist just beneath the lip, a pigeon has built its nest, from which one of the nestlings has fallen. Frantic and helpless, the parent looks down, twisting its head and blinking, as the chick tries to get to its feet, flutters stubby wings, and chirps so softly it is barely audible.

He stands watching a long while before he turns and goes inside.

Someone in the next room, or someone on the radio, someone on TV, is weeping.

# CHAPTER TWO

IT'S HIS THIRD DAY HERE, and he sees in the waitress's eyes that she remembers him. For what he is about, this is the best location, but now he'll have to change.

The man he is watching always arrives within five minutes either side of nine. He parks his year-old Hyundai by one of the skimpy palo verde trees at the rear of the lot. Lunch, he takes at the restaurant half a block away, *Home Cooking* and *Daily Specials* painted in block yellow letters on the front window. Periodically his head and shoulders may be seen in one of the second-story windows. He is among neither the first nor the last to leave.

How this man could possibly be of such concern as to bring someone to engage his services, Christian can't imagine—a nondescript office-dweller at a nondescript accounting firm in a featureless city where everything is dun-colored.

None of that is any concern of his. Interesting, though, that he thinks it.

The client has asked that it be clean, without the possibility of connection, clue, or trace, no indication of professional work, nothing to suggest that it might be anything other than one of the random deaths occurring hourly in cities: drug deals or muggings gone sour, ramped-up lover's quarrels, gang initiations, drive-bys.

Two tables over, a couple is having what his girlfriend back in college called The Talk. Their voices are quiet, their physical interchanges limited to gestures, eyes, and a gamelike shuffling of objects (spoons, glass bin of sweetener, water glass, coffee cups) on the tabletop, but the substance of their discourse is identical to that on the balcony last evening.

Every human interaction, even the most unremarkable, is an economic exchange, he thinks: each side wants something. And it still amazes him how much anger is in people. You see it always in their eyes, in the pitch of voices kept low, in the way they pass through doors or down hallways. So many of them are like jars, forever filling.

He finishes his coffee, toast, and oatmeal and leaves a small tip, pays at the register where the cashier and the other waitress are talking about "classic" TV shows.

On the street a well-appointed homeless man starts toward him, then, with a closer look at his face, something seen there, turns away. Christian steps after him, reaching for his wallet even as he does, but thinks better of it. Too much already, that the waitress remembers him.

There is a small park up the street, just a clump of trees and a bench at street's edge, really, but somehow in this strange place it's even earned a name, Willamette Park, and for two days he's passed an hour or so there following breakfast. He is of an age that no one thinks it amiss for him to be dawdling unoccupied at nine in the morning; with his open-necked shirt, loose khaki pants, and polyester sports jacket, he could easily be a retiree from any of the dozen apartment complexes set in the interlocking streets back off the thoroughfare here. He has not read a newspaper in years, but carries one.

There are pigeon droppings like tides of dried chalk on the bench, so he removes a section from the paper and sits on that. It's because they have no sphincters, he thinks. Birds have no sphincters, giraffes have no voice, dogs see only black and white. So little difference, finally, between an adaptive characteristic and a liability. We all make do. We find ways around.

He cannot see as well from here, but the building with the man he is watching, the building with the name *Brell* set into a fan of bricks above the entryway, remains in his line of sight.

He remembers one of his favorites, the show about cephalopods. Fish were disappearing from tanks in a marine lab. They couldn't figure out what was going on, all these brilliant scientists. The lab was locked, and no one came in at night. The tanks were covered save for a narrow space at the top. Finally they set up cameras, caught it on film. Each night the octopus had been heaving itself out of its tank, crossing dry countertop, and pushing its body through the impossibly narrow opening to treat itself to a midnight buffet from a neighboring tank.

A bus comes by, one of those segmented doubles that looks like a worm. Space for, what, a hundred people within? With maybe a dozen heads afloat in the windows. Its sides bear banner ads for action movies and portraits of local newscasters with too many teeth. He watches the bus work its cautious way around a corner.

Just off the thoroughfare, on one of the narrow, short streets, a car has been parked since he first arrived. Late-model Buick, blue-gray, no parking decals or other stickers, with a single man inside. Lots of dust, but that doesn't take long in this dry, brown place, and the vehicle is otherwise clean. Front plates are not required here, and the vehicle faces out. Though he can't see clearly at this remove, Christian suspects the man is elderly. Light, perhaps silvery hair tops the newspaper he is reading, its color looking close to that of the smoke from his cigars. Likely he's from one of the apartments, out to get away from his wife, or from the family he lives with, from their interdiction of his smoking.

After an hour, Christian has to relieve himself. Two office buildings nearby have bathrooms on the ground floor. He alternates using them.

All these movies and TV shows with stakeouts, you never hear how the guy has to pee in a Coke bottle. He'd done the Texas catheter thing a couple of times in the past—condom, tube, can—but only under duress. Plan well, stay loose, you don't often have to resort to such. Soon enough, anyway, for catheters and their like. Not a chance he'd wait around for that. His old man went that way.

Beautiful young women in business clothes sit on the low wall outside the building smoking, and in the lobby a guard patiently explains why a man in a threadbare black suit and pink flip-flops cannot pass out religious brochures here.

Instinctively the watcher lowers his head as he passes beneath the security camera in the corridor leading down to the restrooms. He checks the other booths, enters one near the door, and sits listening to the sounds around him, some from far away, others close by. Thud and shudder of steel doors closing, clang of feet on mesh-metal stairs, voices stripped of mid-range by high ceilings and hallways. All the breaths going in and out, hundreds of them in dozens upon dozens of rooms, and beneath that, the building's own breath as it pushes through miles of ever smaller ducts.

He looks down at the hand trembling on his bare thigh. He has to pee all the time now. The pills constipate him, despite his tossing back what seems like a gallon of mineral oil a week, and he spends hours on the pot trying, but the pee—the pee never stops.

Toward the end, back when he still lived at home, his father, well along in years (fifty-plus when he was born), would spend afternoons stalking about the front yard, staring at what was left of the city's curb, at remnants of paint on the side of the house, at abandoned bird's nests and tree trunks. He had always believed the old man to be thinking. About how his life had gone, maybe, or the meaning of it all. Slowly he came to understand that the old man wasn't thinking at all, he was searching—looking aimlessly about, with a dull but persistent hope, for something he'd never had.

Coming back up the street, Christian sees activity at the entrance to the Brell building. Three police cruisers and a fire truck sit flanking an ambulance with loading doors agape. As he looks on, attendants wheel out a gurney through the reef of onlookers, who part to make room. One of the attendants is Hispanic, with short, short legs and no hips, his upper body huge, rotund, as though the stuff of his body has been forced upward, year after year, by a belt cinched too tightly. The other, an older black man with a soul patch, woolly sideburns, and not much else by way of hair, holds aloft an IV bag. The attendants bend to release and tuck the gurney's legs as the watcher steps closer.

On the gurney, bloody, patched and pasty white, but still alive, is the man he has been watching.

# CHAPTER THREE

WHEN WAYNE PORTER'S THROAT WAS SLIT, he was thinking about the time he and his friend Joe Weidinger played hooky from Sunday school to climb into the church steeple. They had pushed a table underneath a door in the ceiling of an unused room, put a chair on the table, and climbed into a honeycomb of passageways. The steeple, when they got there, like so much in life, was a disappointment. Bare fiberboard on the interior walls, a *lot* of pigeon shit. And not even a bell, just some electronic gizmo the size of his mom's kitchen radio.

Interestingly, there was no pain, just the sudden gush of warmth, then a feeling as though his body were floating upward, floating away, before the world went dark around him.

Where the hell did *that* come from? Jimmie thought as he woke, heart pounding, to realize that he wasn't breathing. And who was Wayne Porter? His hand had gone instinctively to his throat. He took a breath, looked around. He didn't usually have dreams, and when he did, they were smoky gray and edgeless, washed-out like old movies, not vivid like this. He could remember every color, every angle and surface, every sound. That sensation of sudden warmth across his chest, eyes opening, the face above him already turning away.

Shadows climbed up window and wall as a car passed slowly by.

He'd never been like other children, afraid of the dark, always expecting the world somehow to move subversively against him. He understood that he was simply another object in it, like a rock or a tree. The world didn't care that he was there, and most of the people in it would never know, which was exactly what he wanted. What he needed.

Nor was he in any manner frightened by *this*. But the dream was . . . interesting.

The book he'd been reading last night lay facedown and open on the floor by his bed. *Cities: A Survival Guide*. The cover showed a man in safari khaki peering out from a shower curtain upon which were orange, blue, and green representations of oversize tropical flowers and tall buildings. Intrigued by the title and blurb, he'd ordered the book online, as he did almost everything except food. Not what he'd expected at all, but he had kept reading, his interest modified but still piqued. Over the years he'd read many survival texts from alternative-lifestyle and libertarian publishers. This book wasn't like those, wasn't a survival guide at all, but a how-to to the ways of the city, how to find the best affordable restaurants, where to buy quality clothing for less, access to health care, employment tips—a user's manual to a life he could barely imagine and would never be a part of.

In the bathroom he let the water run till warm, then washed his face. A moth beat at the inside of the window, and as he waited, he eased the window open on its latch to let the moth out.

In the kitchen he filled the small saucepan with water and set it on the stove to boil, rinsed one of the mugs and spooned in sugar, grabbed a tea bag from the open box.

In the front room he stood looking out the window at passing cars, then, with the water at boil and tea brewed, sat at the table. He was up, wasn't going to be able to go back to sleep for a while, didn't feel much like reading. Might as well put the time to good use.

The bills slid all together out of the manila envelope where he kept them in the order they arrived. He turned the stack over and, righting them one by one, began writing checks, duplicating without conscious thought the signature he had worked so long and hard to master. Mortgage, power, gas, water, credit cards. On each invoice he printed check number, date, and amount paid. The third or fourth time he entered the date, something caught within him and he thought: It's been a year now.

At first he had simply waited, living off what remained in the refrigerator and kitchen cabinets, assuming that someone would show up to question the car being gone, lack of activity around the house, his absence from school. By the time he'd run out of food it was clear that he had somehow slipped through society's cracks. One day he walked past the laundry basket into which he'd been throwing the mail and realized there were certain things to which he would have to attend. He pulled the bills, long overdue, out of the bundle. In a hall closet he found a box of checks. In the lockbox under the bed he found papers—the deed to the house and insurance papers among them—with his father's signature. Painstakingly he set about teaching himself to forge the signature—at which point he recalled that it was his mother who had paid the bills, and started over.

For a time, all had gone well. Then a check, the monthly mortgage check, of all things, got returned for insufficient funds. Following initial panic, he'd gone online to the local newspaper's commercial site and managed to sell his father's pride and joy, the

’55 cream-over-mint-green Chevy that never left the garage, the last thing he’d have thought his father would leave behind. There was a tense hour or so when the elderly man came to buy it. He told the man that his father, a nurse at the hospital, had been called in unexpectedly to work, and produced a receipt, signed by his father, for the amount agreed upon online. Wasting no time once the man had left, he ran check and deposit slip to the bank’s ATM site at the grocery store six blocks up Central.

He sold a few more things that way, furniture, his mother’s silver dollars, but he knew it was a dead end and that soon enough, one way or another, he was bound to get jammed up. So without preconceptions he took to skulking on eBay, Craigslist, and a dozen or more local Web listings, keeping an eye out, hopscotching back and forth, buying tentatively, selling quickly at low profit. Misfires and grief early on, but then he had it.

Toys.

Every once in a while some other collectable, lunchboxes in particular, but mostly toys. The market was widespread, huge, and absurd. One day he sold a two-level garage and service center made from tin for $1,200. Pickaninny figures and items linked to TV shows from long before he was born routinely brought in hundreds apiece. Someone in the UK paid $326 for a plastic ukulele that, though in perfect condition, looked as though it had been left out in the sun too long and begun melting.

Prices, though, had been rising steadily, as had (he surmised) the number of those like himself troubling the waters. Already he was looking to sidestep. And while he wasn’t sure of the market yet, still sounding that out, he was thinking hand tools. Adzes, awls, planes, levels, reamers, miter boxes. Woodworker’s tools.

He wrote the last check, entered check number, date, payee, and amount in the ledger, slipped the last check and payment slip into the envelope, sealed it. Then turned the stack of envelopes faceup and stamped each one. Also on each went a sticker from a thick roll:

> James & Paula Kostof
> 1534 Dalmont
> Phoenix, AZ 85014

The bills went back into the manila envelope, which he marked with the date. He noted again, as he always did, that the ampersand, that &, was the largest figure on the sticker.

Still, he wasn't sleepy.

He brewed a second cup of tea and stood at the window. Never much traffic out here after eight or so. A battered truck, white gone gray, swayed by on bad shocks, *Food for the Soul* painted in an arc of rainbow letters on its side with, below that, pictographs of a bowl of steaming food and a Bible.

Sitting at the table beside the window, he clicked on the computer to run his Greatest Hits.

Like Downer Loads with its ever-changing headlines: "Secret Love Nest Found in Abandoned Warehouse," "Sadistic Skipper Drowns Parrot," "Thalidomide Victim Becomes Concert Violinist," "Water Will Kill You." Or his all-time personal favorite, "Coyotes Protect Alien Baby."

Like The Great Illusion America, flogging books, pamphlets and DVDs about the new world order, conspiracies that spiraled back thousands of years, Marines awakening from comas with memories of covert actions on Mars, simple sources of free energy, obtaining New Zealand citizenship, and releasing the secret power inside you.

Like The Real Triangle, which explained how we are being

poisoned by the sea of microwaves washing over us: transmission towers ("500 in L.A. Alone!"), Wi-Fi, cell phones. Put an egg between two cell phones, the home page suggested. Use one cell phone to call the other. Within an hour the egg will be fully cooked.

All of them sites he'd stumbled across one way or another, and now visited daily.

Sometimes as he sat looking out the window, looking into the screen, it occurred to him that he collected the sites—puerile at best, possibly pernicious—the way others seized on Hopalong Cassidy lunchboxes, toy garages, and plastic ukuleles. He didn't understand their attraction, why these sites drew him, but they'd become a refuge.

The best, he always saved for last.

Traveler's comments had started appearing five years before. At first, they seemed just another blog: current events, oil supplies, immigration, foreign policy. Nothing, though, of the entertainment gossip, personal opinions, and political teeter-tottering that filled most blogs. Rarely much about people at all, in fact—just events. Jimmie had checked out the archives, followed the trail backward.

Then things Traveler had spoken of hypothetically—gas shortages, an election debacle, a flood in the Midwest—actually occurred. As the site became progressively more predictive than discursive, Traveler's anonymity moderated as well. *We*, then *I*, came into use, hints were dropped, passing comments that over time coalesced to confession: she was a soldier sent back from the year 2063 on a mission she could not divulge. Interspersed with an oddly impersonal memoir, the predictions continued, some scarily on target, others wildly amiss. Three years to the day after the first blog, following shortly upon an entry headlined "I Haven't Much Time Left," Traveler stopped posting.

Others had kept the Web site going, so that it was now a vast beehive of commentary, speculation, testimonials, exegesis, and silliness accrued about the original postings and growing day by day, even to the point of a biography cobbled together from Traveler's entries, on-site "scholarship," and, it would seem, an imagination spawned of early and ongoing exposure to *Star Trek*.

Jimmie scrolled down the line of recent postings, clicking on those whose blurbs caught his interest, reading a sentence here, half an entry there. Many had quotations from Traveler's entries as epigraphs in smaller typeface above their own.

*When I found Traveler, I was really messed up, stupid, and hopeless. I'm still messed-up, but that's just one out of three. I keep hearing all this "Give something back" and "Make a difference" crap, and all this stuff about how something changed your life, and mostly that's what it is, crap. But it seems to me that Traveler really did give something back, and made a difference. She sure did for me—and my life doesn't look much like it did before.*

*Truth is something you catch only out of the side of your eye; look straight on, and it's gone.*

*When I was 16 I went to my parents and said I had something to tell them.*

*"O my God, you've got little Alice pregnant!" my mom said.*

*"No."*

*"You're gay," my father said.*

*"No. It's worse: I want to be a writer."*

*That same sense of purpose, that I'd discovered my place*

*in the world, my direction, came to me when I found these writings.*

*I came home last night and burned the bed. It's no good without you in it.*

*The firemen are here now.*

*I was a great disappointment to my folks. They had always assumed I'd take over the funeral home that had been in my family for six generations. Instead, I became a doctor. Worked emergency first, then went back and certified in pediatrics. Now I take care of newborns. Some weigh a pound—you can fit them in the palm of your hand. My wife calls them frogs. "How were your frogs today?" I look at them sometimes and wonder what these tiny bodies will turn into (the ones who live), what kind of burdens and disappointments their parents will carry around.*

*"I looked over in the bed where my best friend used to lay."—Willie McTell*

*Truth is, of course, relative. But then, so is relative.*

He scrolled back to a headline he'd passed up before:

*Something had been coming from a long way off for a long time. I always knew that. Then one day I woke up and there it was.*

*"Ride the devil, boy, or it'll ride you."*

Intrigued, he tracked through a slurry of pointless anecdotes, embarrassingly candid memoirs, quotations from popular songs, a half acre of bad journalism and worse psychology, to the original post.

*The first kill, you never forget.*

About rabbit hunting, as it turned out, how the writer and his old man used to go out together in "black Texas woods," how it had made a man of him, but Jimmie was left with aftershocks of the tremor that surged through him on reading that initial sentence.

The sudden gush of warmth, then a feeling as though his body were floating upward, floating away, before the world went dark around him.

The dream, that he'd all but forgotten.

He took his hand away from his throat and went into the bathroom again. The moth had returned to the window, or another one had come, and beat against the glass outside. Briefly he imagined that he could hear the flutter of its wings, but of course he couldn't. He imagined its small mouth making sounds.

# CHAPTER FOUR

HE HATED HOSPITALS.

Probably everyone hated hospitals. And most with good reason: horror stories passed down from generation to generation, memories of helplessness and of pain, their constant reminder of death, like an elbow in the ribs. But he didn't hate hospitals as symbols, for something they represented, he hated them for themselves, for what they were. The entryways that always looked like bad movie sets, the lobbies smelling of cut flowers and overcooked food, the endless din of TVs and overhead pages, the molded plastic chairs, the workers clumped outside every exit smoking.

He'd awakened this morning with his shoes standing like two gravestones at the bed's far end, surprised that he had slept, reaching in those first moments, with a curious mix of instinctive panic and exercised calm, to remember where he was.

Then, lying there still, to piece together the events of the day before.

A call to the hospital had gained Christian no information. Another of the grand paradoxes of contemporary life. Half an hour on the Internet and any reasonably competent skulker could have all manner of personal information about the person he'd been talking to, including his Social Security number. Yet in the name of privacy that person on the phone would not so much as tell him if the man was dead or alive.

"May I help you, sir?"

The woman who had come up on his left had to be at the hard end of her sixties. That leathery skin people out here got, shamble to her walk, spots and runnels on hands and arms. The orange candy stripes made her look like a rapidly aging teenager. There was something behind the ready smile that betrayed her too, a well of sadness waiting there. Her eyes kept slipping to the window ledge, where a family of six Hispanics sat eating from greasy paper wrappers.

He mumbled something about a daughter-in-law, a baby.

"Third floor. Take the second elevator, step off, and turn right. Yellow line on the floor leads to OB, blue to the nursery." She smiled, fleshy hinges below her mouth hanging loose, clearly pleased that some matters could be cleanly dealt with, as her eyes went back to the window ledge.

There were three ICUs listed on the directory downstairs, the largest on the fifth floor, same as the operating rooms, and so the busiest. Where his man, if still alive, most likely would be. And where he himself would be the least conspicuous.

So much in life was about waiting. He took a seat, neither near the entrance nor too far away, in the waiting room, on one of six rows of chairs bolted to steel runners. Automatic double doors opened to the ICU itself; a similar but smaller set, to the hospital corridor. On the remaining walls TVs played, one tuned to a soap opera in Spanish, the other to a talk show whose elegantly dressed older man and scantily dressed young woman pursued with set faces the topic of grief. As he watched, a magician wearing an orange tuxedo replaced the soap opera. On the second TV a man with strawlike hair, face looming above the title of his new book, declaimed "The big bang, we now understand, was not the beginning of everything, only one of those things that happens from time to time."

Through the glass wall he watched a stream of gurneys move down the hall, like planes taking their turn on the runway, to be gobbled up by doors to the OR and ICU.

Grief.

He supposed that for many, grief was like hunger, often spoken of, rarely if ever truly felt.

When he was nine or ten, on a long summer afternoon turning too slowly to evening, he had complained to his father that he was hungry. His old man had looked at him, clock on the mantelpiece ticking loudly. "*Are* you now, boy?" his old man had said. He'd spent the next three days without food. On the fourth his father came into his room. "Now, *that*'s hunger," he said, handing over a tuna sandwich and so ending it. And just as slowly as that afternoon had turned to evening, over the years he'd come to understand that his father's action was fueled not by cruelty but by unvoiced compassion; that the old man wanted him to experience deprivation, to know how it feels to be without the most basic elements of life.

He had read about Victorian women and fainting couches, remembered how in times of emotional stress the black women around whom he'd grown up would (as they called it) *fall out*. But grief? Grief was like the hunger he had known briefly that summer, something you could not get away from, a thing that took you over, wore you, used you.

Onscreen, one of the panelists was crying. The camera moved in for a close up. Her tear was the size of a grape.

Victims, he thought. We're reared and taught to be a nation of victims. Lay the blame elsewhere. All the fault's in the way I was brought up, my parents, DNA, chemicals in my food, some trauma from sixty years ago. Poverty. Racial lines. Glass ceilings. The big bad wolf: society. Two hundred years of that churned out nonstop, what surprise can it be that you wind up with two solid hours of courtroom whining every weekday afternoon on TV, shows about roommates and the awful things they do, people standing in line for talk shows to air their failures and abasements to an audience of like minds?

In the final hours his father had roused from near coma and looked up with a smile on his face. "I'm not hungry," he said, "and I don't hurt." Almost in triumph. His mother had told him that. He hadn't been there, hadn't gone to the hospital at all. He'd been at home, all the lights off but that by his chair, unexceptional music on the radio, reading one of the medical texts he'd collected from secondhand bookstores.

He looked around now, at all these eyes waiting for it to have some meaning. Why she's dying, why their kid got run over or shot, why they had so little time together, why he never took time to tell her so many things. Or maybe just waiting for the end.

He saw them the minute they came in, of course. Knew instantly who they were.

Not kids, the way damn near everyone looked to him nowadays. Both had some years on them. They wore dark dress slacks, the older a white shirt with sleeves rolled up and loosened tie, the younger a sport shirt. No coats. One pair of slacks was neatly pressed, the other baggy with use, its seat so compressed and shiny that it looked like satin. A doctor or nurse came out from the ICU to speak with them, and they followed her back through the doors.

So his man, John Rankin, was alive. And presumably able to talk, since detectives were here.

More waiting, then. More life.

It teemed about him. Children pushing cars with missing wheels up and down the plastic seats, women watching TV with mouths slack, men in denim shirts with the arms cut away, heads tilted back against walls stained by a hundred others. The smell of long-dried sweat and rut, bad food, bad breath.

At that thought, momentarily, he gagged, and felt his bowels flop like a fish.

Then he waited.

Twenty-six minutes by the clock hanging askew on the wall above the doors to the corridor. Focusing through the noise around him, he could hear the clock's quiet heartbeat, see the hand lurch from second to second, catch, release, catch, release.

He waited as the detectives passed beneath the clock, into the corridor, then caught their escort just as the automatic ICU doors swung open.

"Miss . . ." He panted, as though just having arrived. "Could you tell . . . me. Those policemen . . ."

He motioned vaguely, walked to the nearest seat, and fell into it. *Cal Brunner, RN.* She followed him.

"Sir, are you all right?"

Head down, he nodded. In this case, gaining sympathy trumped keeping a low profile. And with luck she wouldn't pause to ask for identification or to wonder how he knew they were policemen.

"Just give me . . . a minute. Those men . . . were they here to see my brother?"

"Mr. Rankin, yes."

"Is he . . . okay?"

"He will be, yes."

"Do they know what happened to him? The phone call . . ."

Again he fell silent, looking up into her face. She sank into the chair next to him, put a hand on his arm.

"You do know he was shot, don't you?"

"But he's . . . they said . . ."

"Yes. He *will* be okay. But he lost a lot of blood. He'll need some mending, some time. Would you like to see him?"

He made a show of breathing deeply. "I can?"

"Of course."

He followed her through the doors, expecting another corridor but finding a large open room half filled with wheeled carts, desktops, and machinery. An octagonal nurse's station stood in the center, patient rooms along the outside. The rooms were triangle-shaped and reminded him of the pie charts they made him cut up back in school, when he was learning fractions. Rankin was in the fifth down. The room was pale green. A steel pan rested by the sink, gauze pads stained brown and yellow peeking over the top.

"Mr. Rankin's fallen asleep again. Best to let him rest. Would you like to sit with him awhile? I can get you a chair."

She did so, and he thanked her.

"I'll be just outside, should you need anything."

Rankin lay still, breathing faster than seemed natural for someone at rest, the skin of his face—all that could be seen—blanched and oily-looking. Four IVs hung above the bed, two of them Ringer's, one blood, the other unidentifiable. An oxygen cannula snaked across the pillow to his nose. The monitor showed his heart rate at 82, BP 100/65, $O_2$ saturation 94 percent.

Sun shone through clouds that had foundered into place outside, giving the sky a bright, climactic cast. He could see, on the inside of the glass, dozens of fingerprints of others who had been here.

How many dead and dying men had he stood above or beside? And death, finally, wasn't all that interesting. What was interesting, what never failed to surprise and amaze him, is the way life always holds on, whatever the circumstances, how it just won't let go. Beetles on their backs with one leg left, and they're using that leg, trying to use that leg, to pull themselves back upright and go on. Men hollowed out by cancer, men all used up, but the body just won't turn loose, and drags them along.

Later he'd imagine that he felt death when it entered the room. He didn't, of course, couldn't have. Nor was he given to fancy. What people often mistook in him for intelligence was primarily an awareness of patterns and correspondences; he'd known that for a long time. And something, some small detail outside his ken but not his consciousness, had changed.

He looked up to the monitors again just as the alarms began sounding.

V-tach.

Then a shudder, the body ceasing breath as Ms. Brunner and another nurse pushed into the room moments ahead of the crash cart.

Walking to the sink, he picked up the business card with the shield on it tucked into the mirror there, and left.

# CHAPTER FIVE

"BREAK A LEG, right?"

He looked over at Graves, who was running his index finger around the inside of a yogurt container. Apparently the spoon couldn't do the job. "Huh?"

"Break a leg—that's what theater people say." Graves licked the finger. "For good luck." The container thunked, dead center, into the trash can.

"Only leg that's likely to break around here is the desk leg from all the case files piled on it."

"Brother, I feel your pain."

"Sure you do. You feel like maybe doing a little work, too?"

"Guess somebody should."

Sayles took off the new glasses and held them out to look at them. He wanted his old ones back.

Business as usual in the squad room. Phones ringing, people walking back to desks dripping coffee as they came, someone cursing his computer. Desk drawers sliding open and shut, bang of a file drawer slammed to. The file cabinets out here looked like something fast-tracked in an auto repair shop: dents halfheartedly hammered out, everything sprayed flat black. The bulletin board that no one ever looked at had memos on it going back to when Jimmy Carter was in office.

"So what do we think?"

"We think it looks like a hit—"

"But it's not, because this guy's not a player."

"As far as we know."

"And because it didn't take. A professional wouldn't drop the ball like that."

"So maybe it's not a hit."

"Random."

"Right. Not a robbery—"

"Or any other clear motive."

After a moment Graves said, "Low cotton."

"Huh?"

"You're living large, they say you're in high cotton. With this, we ain't living large."

He'd given up wondering where Graves came up with this shit, or why he kept saying it. Maybe he had a book of cool expressions, picked out a new one every day before he came in to work. Sayles didn't know, didn't want to know. This wasn't a buddy film, guys knocking off a criminal or two in spectacular fashion then heading back to the house to have dinner together where the wife couldn't cook and the kids were rude and cool in equal measure. One thing he hated, it was people dragging their lives behind them into the squad. That was one thing. Things he hated, it was getting to be a long list.

Josie was still in bed that morning when he left. She'd been in bed the night before when he came home, too. He'd gone into her room with some unbuttered toast, a cup of warm soup, pausing at the door before he went in, out of respect for her privacy. God knows when she'd last eaten.

He sat on the edge of the bed and put a hand on her shoulder. She was burrowed in pretty well. He could see that the pillow was damp with sweat. Across the room, on the TV always left on and at low volume, three white-toothed women exchanged stories about the funny things their husbands did.

"How's my girl?"

She grunted. "That smells good."

"I'll leave it here on the table." He knew it didn't smell good to her, she was just trying to be nice. "Anything else I can get you?"

He waited, and after a minute he said, "Josie, you have to . . ."

She came out from under the covers. She didn't say anything, but she smiled at him, and he felt his heart jump in his chest the way it had when he first met her, the way it had every day for thirty-six years.

"I'm going in to work. Call me later?"

She wouldn't, and he didn't want to call her, afraid he'd disturb the ragged minutes of sleep she managed to grasp, but just saying it made him feel better.

"You're running late," she said, though there'd been no clock in the bedroom for months.

He leaned over and kissed her forehead, catching the smell of her as he did, a mingle of cleansers, mouthwash, alcohol, sweat. Something acrid, sharp beneath. Josie under there somewhere too. He pulled out the trash-can liner, put another in, said goodbye. In the kitchen he tied off the liner and dropped it in the can under the sink.

Standing there looking out, he had drunk the rest of last night's coffee, warmed up in the microwave, now cold again. He thought about his mother, how he hadn't realized anything was wrong until he was a teenager, that other moms didn't go weeks without bathing or refuse to throw away food so that it grew mold in the refrigerator or reuse table napkins. When he was young she always sent him off to school in white clothes. Helped make him tough, he now thought. Third grade, he'd picked up a trash can and slammed it on the head of the class bully for calling him Sailor. After that, he got to like the name. Sailors kept on the move, touched down lightly. Sometimes he still thought of himself as Sailor.

He glanced at the clock. Almost an hour late. He could feel time, every minute ticking past, all the years, crowding against him there at the window, feel the pressure of them in his chest, the weight of them in his bones.

Rankin had been cranked up in bed almost to a sitting position when they entered, looking up with a child's face at the neurologist blathering on about synapses and neural rerouting. Judging by his eyes, the explanations Rankin needed right now were a lot simpler.

The neurologist finished his monologue and, without saying anything more, face as featureless as Rankin's own, turned to leave. The nurse, Miss Brunner, excused herself and followed.

He and Graves glanced at one another to see who'd lead. He stepped up close to the bed, said who they were, held out his shield. Rankin's face made all the appropriate motions, eye contact, down to the shield, back up, but Sayles didn't know how much was getting through. Rankin didn't look much different from when the neurologist was talking. He looked like soldiers did back in country, registering everything, none of it finding or falling into place.

"We have some questions, Mr. Rankin."

"So do I."

"We'll tell you what we know."

"Not for you. The questions, I mean."

"All right. Then why don't we start here: How much do you remember?"

Rankin shook his head without looking away.

"You know you were shot?"

"They told me. I was at work. Yesterday?"

"Three days ago. Today's Friday. You don't remember?"

He looked away a minute, at the window. Sayles wondered why they always do that.

"I remember there were all these faces above me. It was bright, I couldn't see well. And I kept hearing thumps. People talking. My stomach and legs felt warm—like when you pee yourself?"

"Before that," Graves said. "Do you remember anything before that?"

"No, that's about it. I . . . Wait. I was drinking coffee, I think. Taking a break."

"Where was this?" Sayles asked.

"In the break room."

"Second floor, right? Same as your offices?"

"Right. At the end of the hall."

"Which would put it by the stairwell."

Rankin nodded.

"Was anyone else there?" Graves said.

"Maybe . . . Billy. Billy came in, to empty the trash."

"No one else?"

They waited as he shook his head, thought, shook his head again. Nurse Brunner looked in. Sayles smiled at her.

"And you didn't notice, don't remember," he said to Rankin, "anything out of the ordinary?"

"Like?"

"Anything. Doors left open that are usually shut, a change in someone's routine."

It's all about patterns, Sayles thought. You map out the patterns, look for the disturbance in them, the one thing that's not quite right.

"I'm sorry."

"Thank you, Mr. Rankin," Graves said. "We'll need to come back again later, talk some more."

Sayles held out his hand and waited. They shook. "I'll leave a card here on the mirror above the sink," he told Rankin. "Anything comes back to you, day or night, call me."

They shared the elevator with an attendant pushing a man in a wheelchair. IVs of fluorescent-looking yellow fluid hung from poles; a bag almost filled with rust-colored urine swung beneath the seat. As they walked outside, Graves asked, "Where are you?"

He was thinking, of course.

"Of course." Graves looked off. Under a nearby Chinese elm two grackles, feathers shining black in sunlight, were making enough noise for a dozen. "You love this job, don't you, Sayles."

Sayles shrugged.

"Most don't. That surprise you?"

"Not really." Very little surprised him, when you came right down to it.

They got to the car, a Chrysler only a year old and already beat to hell by a hundred wayward drivers. The patrol cars got checked shift to shift and taken care of; pool cars, no one much cared.

"Summer I was sixteen, desperate for money," Sayles said, "I got a job at the slab fields down by the river. Lied about my age, but they didn't care. Not much around in the way of work, it was either that or selling stuff no one wanted in run-down stores. And it paid well. So there I was, hundred-degree heat, bent double most of the day, hauling around crap that weighed as much as I did. Sun slammed down like a wall falling on you over and over, river stank of something huge and ancient and dead a long time."

Sayles fired the car up.

"Now *that's* work to hate."

Under the tree, the grackles making so much noise had been joined by another. Wings spread wide, feathers blown out, two of them were jointly attacking the third.

"Copy," Graves said.

# CHAPTER SIX

SOMETIMES HE IS THERE AGAIN, with the field burning around him, trees at the perimeter igniting one by one, flaring up like birthday candles. Sometimes he hears the *pop-pop-pop* of rifles in the distance set against the *whoosh* of trees igniting, sometimes it all takes place in silence.

He woke in a pool of sweat.

And sometimes he is elsewhere, in the cardboard shipping case that's been roughly stuccoed into permanence, into place. The ceiling is so low that, legs spread and raised straight up, short as she is, her toenails scratch at it. He listens to this, listens to the hollow thump of his head against the wall as he pushes into her, hears the cry of hawkers in the street outside with their vegetables and rice, their twine-tied bundles of lemongrass and herbs and canvas bags of prawns and tiny crabs. She has not said a word the whole time. Two infants stand on tiptoe in a crib made of green bamboo, watching, eyes white as boiled eggs.

He lay awake, still awake or awake again, he really can't tell, staring up at the ceiling, remembering how they all took to calling him Christian because once, as they left a village, he had turned back for a moment and stood with head down. "You praying, Christian?" one of his squad said. He was tired, nothing more. But the name stuck.

He was tired all the time now. The drugs added to it. Fired him up, left him unable to sleep. Made him stupid. And when he did sleep . . .

The worst of it was the dreams. Dreams of things that had happened, of things that hadn't; maybe worst of all, those dreams that took place in some no-man's-land between, dreams of things that had happened but that in the dreaming got twisted, changed.

He shifted in bed, trying to get away from the wetness. A storm was building outside. He sensed the push of it against walls, felt the change in barometric pressure somewhere deep in his chest.

His mother had been obsessed with storms. At the first sign she would lock all doors, secure every window, turn on the radio, later the TV, for a steady feed of bulletins. He remembered one night that she stood for hours looking up at a lone tree on the hill above the house as winds slammed at walls, thunder boomed so hard that the ground itself seemed to shake, and rain pushed in beneath their doors. As though if that single tree, whipping furiously about, were to fall, the whole world would soon follow.

He went into the bathroom to take one of the pills, a whole one this time, and returned to bed. There were no sounds outside, no passing cars. The only light in the room came through the far side of the blinds, where it looked as though a dog had chewed away the outer edges.

Black Dog.

He hadn't thought about Black Dog in years.

Found her in the yard early one morning, a puppy, sick and

covered with ants. Just lying there, looking up at him, him not much more than a puppy himself. Cleaned her, fed her, she got better. And his parents, against their better judgment (an often-used phrase), let him keep her. Always something wrong with Black Dog, though. She slept a lot, ate little, shied away from going outside. Then, when he was ten, eleven maybe, she started to get really sick.

Something else happened then. He'd loved Black Dog as much as he ever loved anything. And as she got sicker and sicker, he grieved, yes. Warmed up bowls of milk for her, petted her endlessly, covered her with an old blanket at night. But something, he realized, had begun to shift. He still fed her, petted her, talked to her. But he had in another sense become an observer, always a step or two apart from the scene, looking on, fascinated at the changes in her body, her eyes. When she died, he was with her, trying to discern the exact moment when life departed, its sign and spore, the turning point at which Black Dog was *there*, then not.

Outside, a car door slammed, there was a shout, then a horn that went on for so long he wondered if it was stuck.

The world speaks to us in so many languages, he thought, and we understand so few.

A couple went by on the walkway outside his room, young from the sound of their voices, and laughing. A bump against his window beyond the blinds led him to imagine them out there arm in arm, hip to hip.

Every time he sees young people it reminds him how distinct are their lives from his own, only the bare outer edges of his world and their world overlapping. Of course he feels that way about everyone; simply more so with the young. People go on, their concerns, their fears, their routines have nothing to do with the world in which he lives, nothing.

A world he is soon to leave.

He wonders what he thinks about that, and realizes that he doesn't know.

# CHAPTER SEVEN

HE HEARD THE FEDEX TRUCK pull in and was at the door before the bell rang.

"How's it going, Jimmie?" Raphael's shaved head glistened. He wore a yellow T-shirt with a picture of a fish and the words CARP DIEM under an unbuttoned uniform shirt.

"Good." Jimmie pointed to the packages stacked by the door. "You?"

"Can't complain. Still above ground, have work, cold beer waiting for me when I'm done. Hey, your dad's been busy."

"He has. Thanks, Raph."

"De nada, my man."

He was amazed that it had gone on so long. That, even with him being as careful and watchful as he was, he'd got away with it.

At first he had waited, living off what was left, canned food, cereal, expecting someone to show up at the door, a neighbor, school officials, police. But no one did. So then, still expecting to be exposed any day, he'd gone on to work with what he had. Now he found it difficult to imagine another life, another way of living. He knew, of course, that this life *would* end, if not in the manner he had first believed. Change was the law, the only law that always applied.

He knew, too, that this feeling, this illusion of permanence, was dangerous.

Still, spend too much time looking back over your shoulder, you never see what's coming at you. Like that story Traveler loved, about the deep thinker who, eyes turned to the stars, kept stumbling over potholes.

Not that he could see what was coming at him anyway. Not that anyone could.

Mrs. Flores lived in the stucco house four down, not quite Pepto-Bismol pink but of that persuasion, with log ends nailed to the outside walls to mimic adobe construction. Mrs. Flores always seemed either to be sitting on the porch, which was swaybacked like an old horse, or working in her garden, which never seemed to grow anything, whenever he walked by, and he always spoke to her. Just hello at first, how are you, but, past weeks, he'd had the sense there was more behind her voice and the way her eyes fell on him. Not that she came out and said anything, but he'd noticed her looking up over his shoulder, up toward his house, as they were talking.

Then, this morning around ten, there she was at the door, holding up a metal pan covered with foil. He never answered the door. Generally people went away. She didn't, but kept ringing, then knocking.

"Enchiladas. Fresh made. I brought green *and* red." She looked around. "Not in school today?"

"I was sick. On my way now."

"Feeling better, then. Good." She held up the pan again. "So maybe I can just give these to your mother."

"She's . . . at work."

She let him take the pan when he reached for it but, doing so, stepped through the doorway. He could tell that, if he turned to go to the kitchen, she'd follow.

"This is really good of you. Thank you."

"Well, you know how it is, all that's involved, you can't make just a few."

"Good timing, too. This'll be dinner. Mom's working late tonight."

"She do that a lot?"

"Some. I'll be sure and get this pan back to you."

"No hurry, I have lots more." She turned, went through the door, turned back. "It's Jimmie, right?"

"Yes, ma'am."

She looked at him a moment and smiled. He wasn't sure he'd ever seen her smile before. "You ever need anything, your folks aren't here, I'm right up the street, okay?"

"Yes, ma'am. And thanks again."

He watched her go, remembering how once when he'd stopped to talk to her in her garden, he'd called her Miss and she had corrected him. It was Mrs., she said. Mr. Flores had gone back to Mexico. Jimmie was thinking that seemed the wrong direction to him, but what did he know. "That man always did the opposite of what made good sense," she went on. "So here I am, alone." And had been alone, by Jimmie's reckoning, close to forty years.

He shut the door.

One of the things he knew was that the day had to have structure. Another thing he knew was that it didn't much matter what that structure was, TV shows that had to be watched, repetitive tasks, to-do lists, small ceremonies, anything. But without that, hours and days and weeks got away from you, nothing seemed to matter anymore, every minute was like every other.

Nights weren't a problem. He slept, his mother always said, the sleep of the young and guiltless. Well, except for the dreams. He'd had another one last night, something about a box, or a shipping crate. And fires. Gunfire. A jungle somewhere.

But his mother had trouble with both. Days with all those empty hours waiting, holes you could fall into. Nights when she'd sweat and speak in a steady whisper and pace the house for hours at a time, turning on lights as she went. One night toward the end when he'd gone to check on her she'd held up a jar to show him, an old mason jar, God knows where it came from, and if you got up real close and looked in, there were mosquitoes in there, half a dozen of them maybe. "It's been a good night," she said. "I've been busy."

She loved straightening things, catching insects, turning on lights, and paying bills. The last year or so, that was about all she did.

He never knew what happened, whether she had left or his father had put her away somewhere, in some hospital or care center. He never asked; they had stopped talking about his mother a long time before. Within the year, his father was gone, too. Jimmie didn't know about that either. Had he just broken and run? Things had been piling up on him for a long time. Watching him, you could see that, the way days and events pressed down, so that it seemed he struggled sometimes just to keep breathing. And if there'd been an accident, if he were dead, then surely someone would have come to the house.

Not that it mattered much. Change was the law. One went on with whatever life one had. When he thought about it at all, Jimmie recognized the legacy his parents unwittingly had given him. Finding his way among the cracks of his mother's oddness and his father's resignation, he had quite early caught on that it was up to him to map the borders and furnish the rooms of a life he could live inside.

When he'd first been left alone, he would sneak out some Friday nights and walk over to the retirement home on Madison. He thought of it as sneaking out, even with no reason to sneak. They had a fish fry every Friday, family night, so there were always kids around, and everyone assumed he was with one family or another, including the occasional resident who seemed to think he was there with them, a grandson maybe. The third or fourth night he'd done that, he met Mr. Burkett sitting at a table with a woman Jimmie thought was his mother but found out was his wife. Mr. Burkett had been in what he called materials management.

"Vendor wanted to be sure he had stock to fill orders, with maybe even a safety bump, he wanted it maintained with no fuss, no bother, I was the one he called. Needed something fast, I had the lines in place . . . You sure you're interested in this, boy?"

Jimmie wasn't, but it kept attention away from him, helped him blend in.

When Mr. Burkett shut the shop down, when his wife got sick, he'd gone into the mail order business on his own, buying in quantity for resale. Toys, shoes, health and leisure products. That sort of thing, he said. And he was as excited to tell Jimmie about this as he'd been about materials management. Where he got supplies, how to package most efficiently and cheaply, how to arrange trades, shipping. All this as he sat holding his wife's hand and feeding her.

Neither of them knew at the time that Jimmie was sitting there at Harbor Rest getting schooled.

And today was Friday. Hospital day, when they'd roll in, or escort with hands cupped on elbows, a dozen or so residents, some with moist red lips, others with skin so parchment-dry it looked as though it would crumble if touched, walkers waiting at idle in a row against the wall.

He'd worked hard at first to try to find what they liked. He'd bring a bag full of books, read a little from each, watch their eyes. They liked stories in which things happened; that seemed to be the most important thing. Travel books, silly mysteries with schoolteachers or grandmothers solving crimes, historical novels, it didn't much matter, as long as events kept moving. They liked best the stories that reassured them the world was as they thought it to be, or as they wished it to be. Children's books and young adult novels always went over well.

"I hope you know how much we appreciate your doing this," Mrs. Drummond said, as she did every week. "It gives them something to look forward to." Every week the same words. Then she'd go on to praise him for never missing a Friday, for being on time, for being such a fine young man. Then she'd go off to wherever her Activity Director office might be, wearing her black suit shiny in the seat and pocket-sprung.

This week he'd brought something different.

Jimmie had quickly caught on that most fantasy, and much popular science fiction, had at its heart some kid—a genius if it was sf, a magical prince or princess unaware, if fantasy—who saved the world. This novel, pitched to young adults, which was bookspeak for adolescents, was a parody of that whole thing. It featured a thirteen-year-old whose parents had mysteriously disappeared, who lives with a family she refers to only as The Strangers, and who feels she never has fit in or belonged anywhere. (That sounded like every kid he'd ever known, Jimmie thought, but never mind.) She just kind of blunders into this face-off between Good and Evil, the last showdown, which takes place right out back of the food court at the mall, and they're so pissed at this kid showing up, they get to rue-ing up one side of the cinderblock walls and down the other and decide to put it off till next time. With the help of another weirdo from school she figures out what's going on, decides that's *not* gonna happen, and spends the rest of book on this mission where, always with the best of intentions and often with near-heroic action, she's just messing up one thing after another, making things worse and worse.

"*Candles for Chance*," Jimmie announced, then the author's name, settling in.

He read in what they called the common room, which was also where the residents ate and which reminded him of nothing so much as his old elementary-school gym that, with folding tables set out, doubled as cafeteria. To the familiar smells of staleness, anxiety, sour food, and sour bodies were added new ones: cleansers, medications, heavy perfume worn by many of the women, the acrid sting of their permanents.

After trying a variety of chairs, Jimmie had settled on a wheelchair that seemed always to be there in the room's corner and never made use of. It had no stirrups, no leg supports. He'd plant his feet flat and roll back and forth in place as he read.

*Someone had put a dead chicken in Carrie's mailbox. Not a real chicken, a rubber one, but still. And it was decidedly dead, with filmy eyes and a floppy beak. She'd gone out there hoping to find the abacus she'd ordered last week. Definitely didn't expect a rubber chicken. Old Mr. Cody down the street had told her about them, offered to show her how to use it if she could find one. They sounded cool, and it took her almost eight minutes on the Internet to locate a source, some guy up in Maine who cut his own wood. His Web site was bottom-heavy with slogans and quotes about getting back to a simpler life, government intrusion and wars she'd never heard of.*

*The chicken was a message, she guessed—but of what? And from whom?*

*Carrie looked around. She saw the mail truck sitting down by the corner, heard the little dog in the house next door (the one that looked like cotton candy according to her dad) yipping.*

*That was Tuesday. Her parents had been missing for a week.*

An hour later Jimmie looked up and saw Mrs. Drummond's face floating at the back of the room, behind his listeners. She appeared hesitant to interrupt, he thought, and when she said "Thank you, James, our time is up for this week," the others protested and begged her to let him go on.

"James has to get back to school," she said. "They excused him just to come and read for you. And it's activity hour now. But we'll pick up there next week, won't we? Let's thank this fine young man."

None of them responded, they just looked straight ahead. Jimmie understood that this had nothing to do with him, that it was the only channel of expression left them. Several smiled as he tucked the book in his backpack and said good-bye.

Wind was rising, sky hazy in the distance, out over Camelback. Most likely another dust storm making its way toward the city. Jimmie unchained his bike, plopped the backpack on the front fender, and wound the straps around the handlebars. The bike was a prize, a forty-year-old aluminum-frame Schwinn in mint condition that had involved a series of complicated trades originating at a vintage bicycle site and spilling through several others.

Over by a tree, three birds with long hooked beaks like thorns raucously did their thing. One repeatedly stepped away, then raced back in with wings spread and head low as though it were flying. Another mainly squawked and jabbered, looking around the way people do when they're making a spectacle of themselves and need to see if anyone's watching. The third just looked confused.

Two men sat in a car nearby, the driver slouched, the other upright, both facing forward, one of them speaking. When the car started up, all three birds froze for a moment. When it pulled away, off the parking lot and past them, the two aggressive birds flew off, leaving the third beneath the tree.

# CHAPTER EIGHT

THING IS, you *don't* forget the first kill. Bodies are messy things. And after that kill, he never looked at bodies the same—not a woman's, not those he turned and walked away from, not his own.

They had fascinated him from childhood. All that wet, heavy stuffing, kidneys, stomachs, bladders of various sorts and sizes, miles of plumbing, pints of blood, the whole of it held in by a bag of skin scarcely thicker than a grape's. How tentative it was, how tenuous a balance. The tiniest well-placed tear, a wandering virus, and it all—in agonizing months, or in an instant—came undone.

Someone had given him, as a child, a *Book of the Body*. The pages were cut into horizontal strips, and as you brought the strips over one by one, a person appeared piecemeal before you: spine, organs, muscles, vasculature, flesh. He couldn't put the book down, and soon went looking for others. By the time he was twelve he knew systems and diseases better than he knew his classmates' names, would walk the schoolyard or sit on the hard gym bleachers with bones and body regions (*tibia, humerus, peritoneum, sclera*) tumbling about in his head. Teachers and parents alike assumed him to be among the rare ones who find direction early in life. At age seventeen he entered college on full scholarship, declaring premed. Two years later he was drinking beer for breakfast as he looked out at rain in mangrove trees and tried not to think about the blisters on his feet. Another jungle there: rich growths of fungus.

They'd gone through the village twice. No dugouts or tunnels they could find, and no evidence of anyone having lived there recently. It was abandoned, only a pig and a few birds dead in the cage remaining as evidence of the generations raised here. Christian had come around the last hut and was almost to the trees when the kid, not more than ten or twelve, sprinted out of them with a swing blade raised over his head. Without thinking, in a single motion, he swung the M-14 around on its strap and shot. The kid exploded—like a dropped watermelon. "Full of gas," one of the older guys told him. "They get that way, from malnutrition, from eating grass because that's all there is. Boy was next door to dead before you ever laid eyes on him." As they moved back into the jungle, he looked up and saw birds circling above the trees. Carrion crows would be first, then others, thrushes, tree swifts, greenfinches, coming to feed on the insects drawn first to the carnage itself, then to the droppings of the birds.

Still awake, he turned his head toward the window, exposing his right ear so that the drip from the tub in the bathroom sounded even louder. The faucet, made of silver-colored plastic, had split, and the drip came not from the tip, but from where the faucet joined the tub; a bell shape of rust and mineral deposits showed it had been that way awhile.

He wasn't accustomed to not knowing what to do.

He was a planner, an engineer at heart, he supposed, not a

creative filament anywhere within him. He thrived on order, on having the next step in place and following it to its conclusion.

A professional, yes—but he'd seen too many professionals to take comfort in the word, too many people who'd lost touch with the simple doing of the thing, the skill, the execution, and had gone off in search of The Big Picture, some grander frame. There was no big picture. Not for this, not for anything else.

The other side of the coin was that what you did, your profession, could so easily become routine, workaday, all pride and pleasure in doing, all feeling, drained away.

You had to find some passage, some *between*.

Windows rattled from the thumping bass of a passing car. Speakers must be the size of Marshall stacks, for that. Music never made much sense to him; he just didn't get it, though as a teenager he listened to all kinds, classical, jazz, rock, trying for a connection, if not with the music itself, then with everyone else, to whom it seemed so important. The car moved away, sound narrowing to little more than rhythm, like distant talking drums.

He didn't know what to do.

Nothing got put in writing. For a time he'd kept it all on one of those personal pocket-size computers, but after leaving the thing behind in a Dallas motel room and barely getting back in time to retrieve it, he stopped. He wrote the details down, only as an aide to memorizing them, then destroyed the paper. Driver's license, passport, Social Security card, all had been obtained under false names. He had no fixed address, received no mail, had no family or acquaintances, paid cash. His life was undocumented. Once he was gone there'd be virtually nothing left behind, nothing to show he'd existed.

The contact had come via the Internet, by referral, as all his work came. He'd tapped in at a cybercafé in San Diego, a place the size of a small barn with tables so far apart the patrons may as well have been marooned on islands.

*I have been introduced to your work by a mutual friend and would like to discuss the possibility of purchasing a custom doll.*

Dolls, because that was what first came into his mind years ago when setting up the system. He had no idea why. He'd always found dolls creepy. An old woman he knew as a kid had a house full of them. You'd look up as you passed through a doorway and one would be staring down at you with rosy cheeks. They were on shelves and windowsills, in glass cases, lined up in polished wooden chairs against the baseboards.

In subsequent days he had bounced the client around various blinds on the Net before directing him to a post office box rented an hour earlier. Three days later he was waiting outside and hit the box with the first rush, walking out, package in hand, alongside women in crisp business dress and old men in ill-fitting pants, polyester shirts, and sweaters. That night just before closing, from a library in Carlsbad, he sent a message: *Your order has been received and is being processed. Thank you for your business.*

Sitting at the particleboard desk in his motel that night, fresh from the shower and still undressed, he began. The desk was pushed up right against the window, overhanging the window ledge and air conditioner vent by inches; meager, barely chilled streams of air blew up to the desktop, then onto him. Kids were skateboarding on the sun-warped paving of the parking lot across the street, riding those small waves. Their cries reminded him of jungle birds.

John Rankin. Fifty-one years old. Worked at a mid-level accounting firm in central Phoenix with a client list of real estate brokers and small businesses, owned an old but spacious and well-kept home in the area where Tempe and Mesa rubbed shoulders. Wife did social services (whatever that meant) at a retirement home. No children. Transplants from the Midwest, one of Chicago's pilotfish suburbs, lured to Phoenix (he surmised) by one of that city's periodic housing booms. Photos had Rankin waist-up in a suit whose coat came close to fitting, sharp-collared white shirt without tie, belt buckle recently let out a couple of notches so that the old half-circle hoofprints showed; Rankin in close-up profile, worried or sleepy, it was hard to tell; and Rankin full face looking bland and characterless, as though he'd just gotten up from a chair and left his personality behind.

Christian looked out at the kids across the street and wondered, even then, as an altercation broke out and the smallest among them kicked off, grabbed his board and swung it two-handed at another, why anyone would want this man dead. The board connected, the big kid went down, and everyone scattered. Thirty seconds later, the lot was deserted save for the kid lying there.

Now, awake in another motel room, in another city, in what seems almost another country, he turned his face again to the window, slowly realizing that there were no lights outside, that the power had gone out.

How long?

He'd taken a whole pill, and when he did that he often slept without knowing he slept, suspended neither here nor there, sleep or wakefulness, dream images drifting in and out of his mind.

The city had grown unpredictably, uncontrollably, spurting within a few years from a modest western city to the fifth or sixth largest in the country. Freeways and streets couldn't keep up; brownouts were common.

Lights flickered, dimmed, flared once, and went out. North and south-southeast, sirens sounded.

So: he thrived on order, on having the next step in place, following it to its conclusion. But what *was* the next step?

His client sat somewhere in a fine house or condo, in a restaurant, in a corporate office, awaiting notification that the doll had been sent. Or, for all he knew, his client might have his own communication lines, might believe that he'd already made the move, and failed.

He had failed twice before, but never like this. Another predator had taken his prey. If there was a way to get close to Rankin now, damned if he could think of it. And with the cops dialed in hard on Rankin, he couldn't stay far enough away.

So what was he to do?

And what the hell had happened back there?

Reason and every instinct within him told him to forget it. Walk. Rearview mirror time. Leave it alone.

Then, it seemed but moments, there was a knock at the door and a voice calling out, "It's checkout time, sir," sunlight strong against the curtains. The bedside clock blinked at 2:36, which must be when the power went down. And checkout time meant it had to be, what, eleven? noon? He had slept, slept soundly, for hours. Now he had only to dress, grab the bag packed last night. Ten minutes and he would be gone, a shadow.

# CHAPTER NINE

POWER HAD GONE OFF during the night.

So, apparently, had Josie.

Home late and soon crashed, Sayles was up at six, straightening things in the kitchen, making coffee and tea, looking out at the leaf-strewn yard. He wasn't much for lawn care, but he'd have to get out there and rake pretty soon, at least pick up the branches and blown-in trash.

He was still wearing yesterday's clothes. Put tea and a slice of Sara Lee coffee cake on the tray, knocked on Josie's door, and waited as he always did before going in.

The bed had been stripped, sheets folded neatly at one corner of the bottom, blanket and comforter at the other. Her bedside table was bare save for a mostly empty tissue box. In the bathroom toilet he found the remains of maybe half a dozen capsules and pills. The rest flushed?

An envelope on the caseless, sweat-stained pillow had on it only the outline of a heart in purple ink.

*I knew you would never agree to it, and would do your best to talk me out of it, so this was the only way I could manage. Please do forgive me. Never have I intended to break your heart. And that is exactly what I am doing.*

*I've had the number of a women's helpline for a long time, and tonight I called. Three came, all of them volunteers who've lost husbands or children, or who are themselves survivors. They helped me pack up the few things I need, helped me to the van. You were snoring as we went out. Another hard day at work, I guess. But aren't they all?*

*I'm not a survivor, Dale. I've known that all along.*

*I don't want to fight this—something you can't understand, it's just not in you, not in your nature.*

*Please give me some time, then I'll be in touch. I'm in good hands, and well cared for. I know you can find me, but I'm hoping that you, like the hospice, will honor my wishes.*

*I love you so much, Dale. You have been kinder than angels.*

That was it. No signature, just another small heart.

Months ago she'd started leaving the TV on all the time, day and night, volume turned down to a whisper. Gave her comfort, he supposed. As though she were not alone. As though there were people in the next room going on with their lives. Leaving, probably because it had become so integral to her environment that it didn't even register, she had neglected to turn it off.

A program about rebuilding a home.

It was one modern equivalent of prayer, he supposed. Things got really, really bad, you sent out a plea, someone bailed you out. A nurse had been shot by a man she'd previously taken care of, who had developed an obsession with her. She was now paraplegic and it was all she and her husband could do to keep things together; even the house was falling down around them. So these group-hug types came in, sent the family off on vacation and, to the accompaniment of rock music, loud shouts and power tools, built them a new house.

"Where are you?"

Sayles surfaced. The screen saver had come up on the computer, a sunset over Camelback Mountain, so he'd been sitting at least fifteen minutes without seeing. Meanwhile Graves had rolled his chair over and sat rocking it back and forth in place, heel, toe, heel, toe.

There are days, Sayles thought, when alien abduction doesn't sound so bad. He exhaled slowly. "What?"

"The thing that's not quite right—like you're always saying?"

"Okay."

"This took some planning, some thought. The guy had to get in there, not get noticed."

"Right. So he was probably wearing a suit, or shirt and tie, looked like he belonged, nothing to stand out—we've been over that."

"He knows where Rankin is, or finds him without difficulty. Seems to know what he's doing. They're alone in there, he has a gun. So why isn't Rankin dead?"

"We—"

"But that's not my point. Look. The gun goes off, Rankin pulls the coffeemaker off the counter as he drops, people are down that hall and in there in seconds. Where's the shooter go?"

"Who knows? Down the stairs. To the bathroom."

"He's just shot a man but he mixes right in, walks away. No

one sees him. That's not a thief, or an angry husband. That's someone cool, someone who's done this before."

"A pro."

Graves nodded. "But he doesn't finish the job. He's not interrupted, it's just the two of them, and he walks away."

Sayles hoped the aliens would arrive soon. He didn't want to be here with Graves. He didn't want to think about Rankin and what happened to him or why or who. Most of all, he didn't want to go home. He hadn't told Graves about Josie, just came on to work like usual. Strength was not about overcoming things. Strength was about accepting them.

Graves started away, then rolled back.

"Something else?" Sayles said.

"Yeah."

"Okay . . ."

"It's lunchtime."

They were almost history, desk papers blowing up in the wake of their departure, when Sergeant Nichols stuck his head out to tell them they had one and they were just absolutely going to goddamn love it.

"Gotta be a pony here somewhere."

Sayles looked at him.

"All the blood, I mean," Graves said. "It's an old joke. This guy—"

"I know the joke, Graves. We all know the joke."

And there was indeed a lot of it. On the bed. Down the side of the bed. On the wall behind. In the slipper beside. Smeared everywhere on the floor.

"Janice Beck," the responding officer said. "Thirty-one, lives alone according to the call-in, a neighbor, but evidence of both a male and a young child."

"Tags?"

"Estranged husband."

Classic tag. Right up there with the live-at-home son, discharged lover, double-dipping boss. Sayles looked over to where Graves stood by the splatter on the wall, holding his hand just over it the way people sometimes do over paintings at museums, moving the hand around. Patterns.

"Recent?"

"Better than a year, neighbor says."

"Child?"

The officer shrugged.

"And no body, Dispatch said."

"Just this." He nodded toward the bed. "Car'd been in the driveway three, four days, maybe longer, no sign of activity. Neighbor came over, no response, called it in."

Sayles looked at the borders of the pool by the bed. "Blood's not that old. Three, four days."

"Starts to congeal in three to five minutes once it's exposed to air," Graves said as he joined them. "Depending on temperature and—"

"Large woman? Small?"

"Five-six or so, by the neighbor's judgment."

"Then, that much blood, it's gotta be better than forty percent of her volume. There's a body. You did the walk-through, right?"

"Right. After we spoke with the neighbor, came in and found this."

"Entry?"

"Took a crowbar to the front door. Locked—back one, too."

"Air's set at sixty-eight," Graves said from the hall. "Dishes washed and in the drainer. Towels, washrags hung neatly in the bathroom, look fresh. Over-the-counter sleep aid, bottle of Claritin that looks almost full."

"Closets?"

The officer nodded. "Clothes, boxes, shoes. Couple of unused suitcases, tags still on them. And no, I didn't touch anything. Eyes only."

Sayles took a closer look, thinking they mostly looked like kids these days. But this one didn't. The odometer had been around a time or two. Fiftyish, but with the attitude of someone much younger. Interesting. "I didn't ask," he said.

"And I appreciate that."

Sayles could hear Graves moving around in the front room. Out the window he watched the officer's partner pace the afterthought of a backyard and alley. His age, mid-twenties, with that brush-cut hair, you could bet on his calling it checking the perimeter.

Graves hollered in, "Lab's on the way."

The officer stepped to the window and tapped at it, beckoned. "You okay with the scene here, Jack and I'll get started on the house-to-house."

"Sure thing. Good job, by the way."

"Not my first time at bat."

Sayles walked to the other side of the bed, opened the drawer of the mismatched nightstand there, shut it, and peered into the space between headboard and wall. Honeycombs of cobwebs in there. The bed wasn't square to the wall. The nightstands weren't square to wall or bed. Even the ceiling looked off plumb, cockeyed. Settling? Or just hasty workmanship?

The floor was laid with tiles from the fifties. Sayles remembered his old man putting down tiles like these in the house on

Fisher Road, covering up what he now knew to be a gorgeous old wood floor. Some kind of sealer that never quite dried, then a paste of black, tarlike goop. The tiles were thick as dinner plates. Had to cut them, carefully, with a knife like Captain Hook's hand, press them in place with a roller that went toe to toe with the old man in weight. Sayles was four or five at the time.

And something now was nibbling at his heels, trying to break through into consciousness.

He paced the room, over to the ancient oak dresser with silver-spotted mirror, no photographs or keepsakes stuck in at the join of wood and glass, back to the bed, to the shelves on L brackets by the door (a bud-shaped flower vase half filled with coins, seven well-read historical novels in paperback, envelopes neatly squared and bound with wide rubber bands, a coffee mug of pens, pencils, and pipe cleaners), peered into the closet and half bath.

Something.

It was the smell, he finally realized, reaching past all the blood, through all those years.

Camphor.

Mothballs.

He stood by the cedar chest in the room's corner remembering the one his mother had when he was a kid. He didn't know what happened to it, it wasn't there by the time he was puttering about the house on his tricycle, but he remembered the smell. The chest was filled with sweaters and heavy clothes they never wore, linens and towels kept for guests they never had. And it was forbidden to him.

Beneath the cushions atop, it apparently having served as a makeshift sofa, the cedar chest wasn't quite closed, and the smell, the camphor smell, was coming from within.

Sayles removed the cushions and opened the chest knowing what he would find. It was a small chest, too small. There were marks on her torso where the killer had knelt on her to force her body inside. Her neck and arms had been broken in the process. Later they would find the child's body below hers. The child had been alive when put into the cedar chest. He had died of suffocation. Both of them had smiley-face stickers on their foreheads.

# CHAPTER TEN

HIS FEET WERE ON FIRE.

He had no idea where he was. He could see the sun low through the trees. The last thing he remembered was the sound of heavy artillery, the *thwack* of chopper blades. Now it was quiet. Scattered bird calls high in the trees. Rumblings far off that could as easily be firepower or a storm building. In his sleep, if it was sleep, or maybe before, he'd pissed himself. He pushed up on hands and knees, and insects went rattling away from him through the ruff of dry leaves.

Letting himself fall back over, he rolled and slowly pushed with his hands into sitting position. The dizziness passed, but he still was not seeing clearly; everything upon which he focused, trees, the burned-out stump beside him, his boots, had two or three borders. It took a while to get the laces undone, the phrase *Died with his boots on* running stupidly in his head the whole time.

At first he'd thought it was leached color from the olive canvas boots. Too green, though—and growing. Alive. He remembered a photograph that an uncle had showed him of his house in New

Orleans, sidewalk, wood, even cement blocks covered with a patina of green. The growth on his feet went from green to black. No idea what part was fungus or mold, what part rotting skin. He didn't want to think about that. But his feet itched like mad and burned like fire.

His socks were soaking. He swung them in circles, pushing out as much wet as he could, wiped between his toes with a handful of leaves, put socks and boots back on, and, hand against the burned-out trunk, experimentally stood.

—And woke, *What the hell?*, instinctively swinging out of bed to put his burning feet on the floor, toes curling around the carpet's nap.

The clock blinked at 2:35. Jimmie walked to the window and looked out. No lights anywhere. The storm, he supposed. But he had slept through it. His heart still hammered. Strange how quiet it was, sounds so familiar as ordinarily to go unremarked now conspicuous in their absence: box fan wobbling and gently bucking near the door, that faint buzz of wires in the walls, hum of the refrigerator two rooms away.

He hadn't returned the pan to Mrs. Flores yet. Why he thought of that now, he didn't know. Why he hadn't done it, he didn't know. He'd scrubbed the pan, dried it; it had been sitting on the counter since.

Something else he was supposed to do as well . . .

The storm had long passed. He watched a police helicopter circle in the sky over toward Black Canyon Freeway, its spotlight lashing in crisscross patterns. Power came on—he heard the click of relays in the cooling system, felt a brief whoosh of breath from the fan—then again shut down. He'd fallen asleep without shutting off lights, and they had come back on just long enough that his eyes had to readjust to the darkness. As they did so, and as stars came back into the sky above, he remembered.

The telescope.

It was supposed to have gone out days ago. He' d bought it from a woman in Texas whose grandfather had recently died. Produced by a company that, originally a processor of 3-D films, had surfaced briefly in the fifties to send into the marketplace a stream of high-quality, low-cost optical products—microscopes, binoculars, reading glasses, prisms—the telescope shared its birth year, 1957, with Sputnik. And the Seattle-based collector of all things Sputnikian would be wondering where his expensive telescope was.

Very unlike him to forget things like this, not to follow through. Maybe those dreams were having a greater effect than he realized. Taking their toll. He'd have to send an e-mail to the buyer right away.

Automatically, he went to the computer and hit the switch. Nothing. Of course. No power. And standing there, for a moment he felt something he couldn't at first identify, then knew to be panic—occasioned, he initially thought, by his lapse. But the veil fell away, and he came to understand that the feeling was something more elemental: panic at being out of touch, at having his connection to the world torn away.

The moment, the feeling, quickly passed, but a shadowy residue, like an afterimage, remained.

When the lights flared back to life, he stood there blinking.

# CHAPTER ELEVEN

FOUR YEARS AGO he'd hit a pothole.

Man's name was Les Baylor, and he worked midnight shift at a hospice, there for most of his adult life, twenty-some years. His routines had been simple to track because they were just that, routine, hard and fast. Lived in an unadorned, unkempt, underpopulated apartment complex eight blocks from the hospice. Stopped off at the Recovery Room for a beer on his way home when working since the Recovery Room opened at six A.M., walked up that way most late afternoons for an hour or so. Two, three beers was his limit. Breakfast he took at the hospice cafeteria. Every other evening he visited Blackhawk Diner for the special of the day; the rest, he dined at home on sandwiches and the occasional order-in pizza.

After it was done, Christian stood in the apartment looking around. Such a bare existence had gone on here. No television, maybe a dozen library books long overdue. Three radios, one for each room including the bathroom. Jeans, shirts, and scrubs folded and kept in layers on steel shelves in the single closet, socks and underwear left jumbled in a laundry basket beneath.

No medications in the bathroom, only toiletries, comb and brush, safety razor caked with mineral deposits. In the kitchen, bags of health-food cereal, a keglike container of orange juice, cheese and cold cuts, mustard, milk, dark bread.

Simplify, simplify.

He shouldn't care, of course, or stay around to ask questions. It was done. And strangely enough it wasn't the why of it that rattled about his head, but the who of it. The man lying on his bed as if asleep had taken up little enough space in this world. He worked, he ate, he slept. Listened to the radio, one would have to suppose. Had no family and no apparent friends aside from a couple of fellow workers who occasionally joined him at the Recovery Room after shift.

The reason, the why, belonged to the person or persons who arranged this gig. But what of the man himself, Les Baylor? Had he left so much as a shadow in crossing this world? And what could the shape of that shadow have been, for someone to want him dead?

Christian poked at the clothes, picked up shoes to look at their laces and soles, shuffled through bills and recent mailings on the desk, which was particleboard, crumbling back to sawdust at the nearest edge. He turned each radio on. Two set to classical music, the other to easy listening.

He found the 8x12 brown envelope marked *Accounts Due* sitting on edge behind the library books. One leg of the metal clasp was gone. He thumbed it open, looked briefly, and took the envelope with him.

Back at Hacienda Motel he opened it again, slid the contents onto a table not unlike the one in Baylor's apartment. Atop sat a composition book, the kind with marbleized covers, containing names and short biographies, close to a hundred of them, he figured, one per page, the thing so dense with entries that it was twice its original thickness.

*Dav Goodman, born 1919, gunner in WW II. Worked as a salesman, cattle food initially, then hardware and, finally, furniture. Retired when Parkinson's hit. One daughter, lives up in Iowa somewhere, not in good health herself. Son died "a few years back."*

That went on for some time before ending "Died April 9, 1998," a formula that continued throughout.

*Shelba Adari, born 1988. A runner on SMU's team until the day she fell on the track while training and they discovered that her tibia had broken. Cancer, which was soon everywhere. Patrick, the law student she'd been engaged to, came to see her every Friday.*

"Died Friday, December 21, 2005," that one ended. The dates of death were written in a different ink from the other entries, an unusual green color, almost emerald.

Also in the envelope, behind the composition book and clipped together with a well-sprung paper clip, were a sheaf of letters written on a variety of paper. None had address, date, or salutation, though some bore a single letter upper left.

*K,*

*There is so much pain in the world. I don't know how we stand it. We reach out for the bag of food pushed through the take-out window and somewhere an entire town is being destroyed, bombs are being driven into shopping malls in old Toyotas, children are dying of hunger.*

Outside his motel room window, across the street, stood a strip mall. *That* could be bombed out, he thought, from the way it looks. Of six storefronts, only the end one, a convenience store, remained in business, the rest caving in upon themselves, windows cataracted with dirt, bird droppings, and spray-paint tags. A young woman sat on what remained of the sidewalk outside the convenience store, back against the wall, talking on the pay phone.

*D,*

*When I was eight or nine, on a road trip to visit my grandmother in Pine Grove, we came across an accident that had just happened. An old truck with no fenders had gone off the road and turned over. The driver, who looked ancient to me, like the gimpy old bearded man in cowboy movies, was trapped under the doorframe and when he finally pulled himself loose, about the time we got there, most of his leg stayed behind. While my father was busy improvising the tourniquet that saved his life, I sat by the little girl with my hand on her forehead. She was a year or two younger than me, couldn't possibly be his daughter, I thought, old as he was. She died, with my hand on her head, just as my father finished his work and looked up.*

*We do what we can to ease another's pain, thinking it will ease our own. But it doesn't. Somehow, instead, it adds to our pain.*

*We don't erase theirs, we take it to ourselves. Is it possible that, far beyond our understanding, balances are at work? That suffering is like matter in the universe, there is only so much of it, forever the same amount, and all we can do is rearrange it, pick it up here, put it down there?*

*K,*

*Everything comes at a cost, even the good we do. Dav, Mr. Dahlhart, Belinda Chorley, Jerry ("Not the President") Ford, Joe Satcher, they're all at rest now, where pain, hunger, fury, even their own infirmities, cannot reach them. Angels didn't lay them away like in the old song, not the angel of death or any other angel, because there are no angels. It's all on us.*

*We have to be our own angels.*

*A man named Mr. Sheldon was the first. His heart, long overburdened by emphysema, was at last giving out, his skin by then mostly blue and parchment-like and looking like a drying mud flat, all cracks and fissures and discoloration. He had been a heavy equipment operator and "built half this state's good roads." He had one daughter, severely retarded. ("You think it was my drinking done that? I was a heavysome drinker those days.") She visited once a month, first Friday, with her son, who seemed to be her caretaker. At the end, when I was there by him and Mr. Sheldon understood what was happening, he told me to call him Billy.*

*Even the hero, even the superhuman, exercises power at a cost. Terrible weakness, all but unbearable pain, inordinate aging.*

*Exile. Madness. The gift he is given, and what he gives in return, sets him forever apart.*

*Cost.*

*And eventually the bill comes due.*

There were, all told, sixteen letters (if indeed that's what they were), some written straight out, others with deletions, changes, inserts scribbled between lines or sideways in the margin. Christian started at the beginning and read them all again, wondering who they might have been intended for, sensing a pattern, or hoping for one: some coherence, a line.

Not a time he'd easily forget. That month, following hard on weeks of increasing pain, blood in the stool and frequent vomiting, sitting in a brightly lit room that looked to be little used, surrounded by blond furniture, he'd learned the name of what was slowly taking him over and down.

Four years. He had beat the odds.

Beating the odds was it—all we could ever hope for.

That time, to his message *Your doll has been sent* he received no acknowledgment or reply.

And that night, the city around him was beginning to burn—a fire that had started in the industrial area just south of the city's center, in a meatpacking plant, and quickly spread—though he wouldn't know it till days later, far away in another town and another motel room, from TV news. He had been watching a show about vultures.

They're not birds of prey, a zoologist said, but birds that clean up the messes around us. They can ride air currents for hours without once flapping wings, detect a dead animal by scent from two hundred feet in the air. Their intestines digest and destroy agents of such diseases as cholera and anthrax in the carcasses they devour. No chase or frenzied kill here. The vulture keeps watch, waits patiently for a day or two until gases start to leak from the decomposing corpse. One type, the bearded vulture, even specializes in bones.

The zoologist had mutton chops so bushy and thick as to draw one's attention again and again from his eyes and face. Christian remembered how those eyes glistened as the man explained that, to make their meals more interesting to the birds, zoo attendants wrap freshly thawed rat carcasses in paper tightly tied with twine.

# CHAPTER TWELVE

NEXT TABLE, which was about hips-width away, a man in shorts and T and a woman in a freshly ironed cotton dress, both fiftyish, were discussing their relationship over yellow mugs of high-end coffee. Against the wall behind them, two young men in dress slacks, white shirts, and ties glanced up from their computers, spoke briefly to one another, resubmerged.

He looked at the card again.

Rankin had been moved to a regular room that morning. Christian, sitting in a chair nearby, seemingly lost in a book bought at the gift shop downstairs, had listened as an X-ray transporter reined his gurney up at the nurse's desk to check in. "Here for Rankin, room 543, right? Chest, PA, and lateral?" Minutes later the laden gurney rolled by.

Christian stood and stretched. He laid his book open facedown on the chair, walked toward the bathroom, then took the turn into the hallway, pulling out a clipboard he'd found in a supply room and kept under his belt at his back.

Room 543 was halfway down the hall on the left. Nodding to housekeepers conferring at their cart, one Hispanic, one Korean, he held up the clipboard and went in.

The room smelled of cleansers and disinfectant. Sunlight, awash with dust motes, streamed through the wide-slat blinds. A tissue clung to the side of the otherwise empty trash can at bedside. Stains on the bottom sheet: brown for blood, yellow for Betadine, red or purple probably from spilled foodstuffs. Pillow oily and ripe with sweat, half a dozen dark hairs adrift on it. Ringers and a broad-spectrum antibiotic hanging, shut off for the trip. He'd have a hep lock, maybe a central line.

The TV in the next room went off. It had been all laughter and loud voices, one of the Spanish-language channels. Now other sounds moved in to fill: the gurgle of the toilet whose ball valve didn't quite fit, the all but inaudible hiss of oxygen leaking from the room's piped-gas coupling.

Nothing bearing witness to the man who occupied this room. Not the blood-smeared clothes in which he'd arrived; cut off him in ER, they were a crusty wad in a plastic bag on the floor of the closet, scarcely recognizable anymore as clothing. Not the misbegotten stack of magazines on the window ledge, *Field & Stream*,

*Money, Star Talk*, brought him by well-meaning volunteers. Not the toothbrush at bedside, standard-issue institutional, clear plastic, twelve dozen to the case. From similar cases came the blue drinking cup with emesis basin and urinal to match. The urinal unused, since Rankin was still catheterized.

Christian had registered the footsteps when first heard, followed them with increasing portions of his attention as they became louder. He was standing by the oxygen outlet as a man stepped into the room. Christian bent close to the coupling as though to read something from it, made as though to scribble another something on the clipboard. Then turned to show mild surprise.

Steel-gray suit, blue dress shirt, leather loafers, and belt. Hair light brown and worn longish. Hands muscular, veins and tendons clearly visible.

"You're not, I take it, Mr. Rankin?"

"Mr. Rank— Oh, the patient, you mean. That's in here? Nope. Just doing my day's work." He brandished the clipboard. "Routine check of zone valves. That carry medical gases?"

"Of course," the man said, though everything beneath the surface, posture, expression, tone, belied that.

A cop, Christian would have thought, but that wasn't a cop suit. An easy athleticism about him, too, the way he moved. Doctor? Hospital official maybe. But he wasn't wearing an ID badge the way all other employees were. Christian wasn't either, of course.

"Mr. Rankin is . . . ?"

"Search me." Christian tilted his head back toward the wall. "Gases? Pipes? Probably down for tests, PT, like that."

"Yes, I suppose so."

"You could always check at the nurse's station."

"Of course."

The man stepped to the side to allow him to pass. Christian didn't glance back but knew he was being watched as he moved down the hall, away from the nurse's station this time, to the stairway entrance. Remains of cigarettes on the first landing, a plastic cup that had served as ashtray. Hightop tennis shoe left behind on the next. One very confused sparrow perched on the sill trying to see out the frosted glass.

So the eyes-on was a bust. The sole thing of interest he had was what he'd carried away on his first visit.

This calling card.

The woman in the freshly ironed dress at the next table stood, saying "I'm sorry you feel that way, Charles." She dropped her cup in the trash can by the door on the way out. The man sat watching as she walked to her car, a silver Volvo, got in, and pulled away. Then he looked quickly around, and left himself.

Sayles would be one of the cops he had seen outside ICU. More likely the one with well-worn, baggy pants. He'd be senior officer, be the one to leave the card. Past caring overmuch what impression he made. Work clothes for him, nothing more. Just get the job done.

Easy enough to check out. Call the station from a pay phone, say he had information, ask to be put through to the investigating officer. Maybe even pull vitals or a photo off the Internet—directories, newspaper archives, and the like.

That left the visitor back in the room. Who hadn't appeared to know Rankin on sight, but it was hard to tell. Maybe a doctor or hospital employee, as he'd first thought. Someone from the business office, a PA or nurse practitioner, chaplain.

But maybe someone with a more exacting reason to seek out John Rankin.

. . .

Two days later Christian is in the half-alley running behind Sayles's house. Having decided he can't let this go, he's sniffing the wind. No way he's getting near the police station, and he wouldn't be able to learn much of anything if he did, but maybe Sayles brought his work home, maybe there's a notebook, files.

Sayles pulled out of the drive thirty minutes back. In his dress shirt, tie, and baggy slacks. Heading in to work.

Eleven ranchstyles lined Juniper Street, most of them white or some shade of brown, distinguishable one from another primarily by the level of disrepair. Spiny, garish limbs of bougainvillea soared above rooflines. Grass and weeds flourished in cracked driveways and at curbside.

Sayles was thoughtful enough to have a fenced backyard, a great boon to the enterprising B&E-er wishing to go about his job unseen. It took five minutes, tops. Sliding glass doors of the patio had pipe in the inside runners, windows appeared to be nailed shut. But the narrow door to the utility room didn't quite meet the casing; its lock popped when he ran a knife blade in. Chances were excellent that he'd be able to come out the same way and reset the door, leaving no trace of his visit.

Interestingly enough, the living room looked to be used primarily as a place to sleep. No litter of glasses, food, newspapers. Just blankets folded and stacked at one end of the couch with a pillow atop them. The bedroom, on the other hand, looked as though it were waiting for a photo shoot, bed made, everything in place, white tile gleaming from the small bath beyond.

Woman's house, no doubt about that from the shelves of figurines and trinkets in the living room, curtains, matched furniture, reproductions of paintings on the walls. None of it recently dusted, though. And that bedroom looked unused. Some unusual smells behind those of cleansers and a plug-in room freshener.

The kitchen was getting most of the action these days. A little settlement of cup, coffeemaker, coffee can, and measure on the long mesa of counter. Two-cup pan and lid, bowls, spoons in the drying rack by the sink, four cans of Progresso soup in the trash. Couple of bottled beers, jug of water, cold cuts, and eggs in the refrigerator. Half the cold cuts missing and the rest in need of medical attention. The eggs were two weeks past sell-by date.

The table meanwhile had gone home office. Bills removed from envelopes and in a neat stack, checkbook as paperweight. Not a lot of interest in the checkbook entries—the usual City of Phoenix, APS, Qwest, Southwest Gas, two credit cards—except for the medical. Man paid bills on time and, when he could, in full. Monthly partials, though, to two doctors, an online pharmacy, and Good Samaritan Hospital. Occasionals to LabCorps and a medical imaging firm in Tempe.

That accounted for the missing woman and the smells in the bedroom. Also for the balance of $376.92 in the account.

So where was she? Not dead, or there'd be indications: photos, service card, sympathy cards, mortuary bill, deposit check. Back in the hospital, then?

A pocket-size leather-bound notebook sat beside the bills and checkbook, Sayles's name embossed in gold on its cover. Christian opened it. The single entry was on the inside cover, *From Josie, Christmas '04.*

A third of the pages were missing from the legal pad alongside. The topmost of those remaining had a listing in Sayles's handwriting of hospices in and about the valley. That page, with others, had been rolled back and tucked under.

*J. Rankin*

*Louis = nothing*        *Hector alerted*        *G ? out of town*
*A cipher*    *shooter's a cipher*

*non-lethal!*

*accountant*    *0 military*    *married*
*midwest—how long out here?*

*Check with organized crime units*    *FBI*    *??*

*Barrow says it's like those lawyer jokes, someone's going after accountants, one at a time.*

*Hector: Nothing to hold onto, he says, but.*

*<u>Dolls</u>*

That was the page showing. And not good.

Christian stood looking back at a photo on the refrigerator, the wife he supposed, the missing woman, with a copse of bamboo behind her, holding a snub-nosed monkey.

Bending over the legal pad, he wrote:

> *Please contact me. This is for you alone.*
> *I sell dolls.*

He added one of his e-mail addresses.

# CHAPTER THIRTEEN

"YOU DOING OKAY, though. Right?"

"Fine. Police were here?"

"I saw them in the front yard and came on over, to be sure you were all right. Someone reported a prowler in the neighborhood."

Mrs. Flores had waved from her porch and started toward Jimmie when he turned onto the street.

"They weren't trying to get in the house?"

"Checking yards is what they said. Just going down the line."

Pausing at the door, he said, "If you'll wait, I can get that pan for you," but she followed him in and stood by the front door. He went to the kitchen and came back with the pan. "Sorry it's taken so long to return it. The enchiladas were great. Delicious."

"Your mother doesn't cook much?"

"Sure she does. But not Mexican food."

"I could show you how to make them, just the same as me, if you're interested."

"Thank you."

Her eyes had been glancing around the room. Now they met his.

"How long have they been gone?" she said.

"What?"

"Your parents. How long?"

"They—"

"Lots of people don't notice what doesn't have to do with them. Some do. I've suspected for a while now. You're a smart boy, you've done good." She shook her head. "People up here baby their children so much. But don't worry, no one will hear it from me. Where I come from . . ." She didn't say anything for a moment. "The way you're brought up, the way you think, a lot about that doesn't change. But listen."

"Yes, ma'am?"

"You need anything, you have a problem, whatever it is, you come to me, okay? Can you do that?"

"Yes, ma'am, I can."

"That's good."

"Thank you, Mrs. Flores."

He watched her go down the walk, thinking how she got around like a much younger, much thinner woman than she was. Back on the porch, in her rocker, she waved and bent over to retrieve her glass of iced tea. Jimmie went inside, picking up the scatter of mail by the door. A thick 4 × 8 envelope remained lodged in the mail slot, and he looked at the return address, typed, cavities of the *o*'s and *e*'s dark with old ink. Slowdown Time, a collector's site and occasional supplier, and one of the few to still put out a print catalog.

Hungry, he went into the kitchen and poured a glass of milk. He was standing looking in the refrigerator when he heard floorboards creak.

Someone was on the back porch trying to look in. They

couldn't see much, of course, not with the tight-gauge screen door and curtains. But they shouldn't be there. She shouldn't be there.

A woman.

Who now had stepped off the porch and, hands cupped around her face, was trying to see in through the windows above the sink. Her hair was gathered on top somehow.

She tapped on the window.

"Hello? I can see you in there. James—is that you?"

Someone who knew him, then. Or knew about him. Someone who had come looking for him. A tumble of thoughts went through his mind, none of them good.

First the police, now this.

When he opened the door and saw her, he knew. She'd changed, but not that much. She looked younger than he remembered. Had on loose jeans, a T-shirt with a dressy jacket over it, flat-heeled black shoes. He remembered the hair thing now, a French twist, she always wore her hair like that when she got dressed up. There seemed an odd lightness to her.

"Jimmie? Is that you? My God, how you've grown!"

He stepped back from the door, and she came in. Limping? Favoring her left leg, at any rate. She reached up to smooth her hair. Nails cut short, not long the way he remembered them.

"Where's your father? Where's Jim?"

"He's not around."

She took a glass out of the cabinet, ran it full from the tap, and turned, leaning against the sink. The glass was one of his from when he was much younger. It had bears on it.

"I guess I can't hope that you're glad to see me. But it sure makes me smile to see *you*. You look good, Jimmie."

She drank the water in one long swallow.

"You're in, what, the eighth grade now? High school?"

"Something like that."

"And I bet your grades are good."

After a moment he said, "Why are you here? What do you want?"

"I did want to see you." She rinsed the glass and put it in the sink. "But I need to talk to Jim, to your father."

"After all this time."

"It's not really that long, Jimmie."

"And you two haven't been in touch?"

"Why would we be in touch?"

He looked away.

"Jimmie . . ." She took a single step toward him. "What was between your father and me, it stays there, okay? Between us."

"If you say so."

"Is he still working at Ralph's? I can swing by there. I have to be getting back pretty soon."

"He's not there."

"Okay. Where, then?"

"You think you're the only one who can leave?"

She looked around, a scatter of visual clues coming together behind her eyes. "It's just you, isn't it?" she said.

Jimmie nodded. "He didn't stay too long after you . . . left. Went away. Whatever you did. It's been a year now."

"And you're okay? How did you get by? What are you living on?"

"I sold your silver dollars."

"My what?"

"Your silver dollars, the ones your grandfather gave you. In the bottom of your chest of drawers. And Dad's car. And some other things."

"I'll bet you did. Oh, Jimmie! What have we done, how did this all happen?"

"I'm okay with it. I'm good."

"So it would seem. The need for parenting is obviously overstated. Not that you ever had much of that."

She took another step toward him, saw him struggle to avoid instinctively stepping back, and stepped back herself.

"You don't know where James has gone, then? He hasn't written, called?"

"No idea."

"Well . . . I guess that either complicates things or simplifies them."

She had idled about the kitchen and now stood by the refrigerator, finger lightly on a sheet of composition paper layered with faded crayon. Buildings jutted dark-eyed above empty streets. The entire upper third of the sheet was heavily scribbled with black. He had held the crayon on its side and pushed hard, back and forth.

"I remember this. You'd seen some movie on TV, aliens who looked like giant rutabagas come to destroy the world. They started taking over people's minds, one by one. You drew this the next day and told us '*This* is how it's really going to happen.' You were five. As you got bigger we kept moving it up on the door. Now just look where it is."

She went back to the window. "And look where *we* are." Then, turning, "I can't stay, Jimmie. But is it okay if I come back from time to time? When I can?"

"If you want to."

"Good. I'll see you soon, then. You take care of yourself. But that's exactly what you have been doing, isn't it?"

He stood inside the door after she left, looking out into the bare backyard. Had he really played out there? It seemed so unlikely, or so long ago. He saw that the screen on the door was pushed in at the bottom. He'd have to fix that.

[illegible]

[illegible]

[illegible]

[illegible]

[illegible]

[illegible]

[illegible]

[illegible]

[illegible]

[illegible]

[illegible]

[illegible]

# CHAPTER FOURTEEN

DOLLS.

What the hell did dolls have to do with anything?

It had come up in talking to Hector, his usual he-maybe-heard-someone-heard that was half the time garbage, the other half incomprehensible, with once in a great while a tiny sliver of something substantial stuck between. Then when he got home from his shift and from sitting in his car outside the hospice for over an hour, watching shapes and shadows move around inside the windows, there it was, on the pad: *Please contact me. This is for you alone. I sell dolls.* He'd mixed a drink and sat down to go through his notes.

Dolls.

And now he found himself looking at that sunset over Camelback again. Thing had been getting lots of screen time of late. Graves was off testifying at a hearing, guy they'd finally busted for ag assault after giving the poor SOB, a vet, three walks. This time they hadn't been able to smooth it over, and truthfully hadn't been much inclined to do so.

Down the row between desks, Robert came plodding with his cart and his earphones plugged not into an iPod but into one of those pocket-size transistor radios you never saw anymore, one he'd had, he kept telling everyone, since he was a kid. The mailman, even though no one got mail anymore. Mostly Robert passed out memos and requests for donations and the like, and those things that *were* addressed to specific people, he generally got them wrong. His father had worked the job for nineteen years, had five months to go till retirement and pension before he made a routine traffic stop, got slammed with the door then run over four or five times. Didn't even make it to the hospital. Right after that, the chief gave his kid this job and he's had it ever since, going on ten, twelve years now. Robert's around thirty.

Sayles thanked him and looked at the envelope Robert had handed him. He'd take it over to Barry Vandiver later.

Robert, always a steady-rolling, keep-it-moving sort even with nothing to do, which was most of the time, lingered by Sayles's desk. Sayles watched him pull out the earplugs and carefully place them in his shirt pocket with the radio.

"You got a minute, Detective? Can I ask you something?"

"Sure thing." He pushed a chair a couple of inches Robert's way with his foot, but Robert remained standing.

"I don't know what to do," he said.

"Okay."

"I found something, and I don't know what to do." His eyes met Sayles's and slid away again. "I was looking for something I just up and remembered, a shirt my dad used to wear, pretty blue one with red roses, I thought it might fit me now. All his things are in the closet in the other bedroom."

After ten or twelve years? Sayles thought.

"But I couldn't find the shirt at first. It was all folded up in a plastic bag from the cleaners, with some dress shirts, in a box on the top shelf. This was in the box, too."

Robert held out a slim notebook, the kind a lot of cops use for taking notes at the scene. It came from the same pocket he kept the radio in. Sayles took it and looked at the first page, then leafed quickly through. Names in one column—mostly initials—with dates and sums of money. Little doubt what this was. Thousands upon thousands of dollars over the years.

Sayles looked back up at Robert. Did he know? Always hard to tell how much Robert understood about things. Couldn't read it in his eyes, his face. A glimmer, maybe. A suspicion.

Most people, when they ask what they should do, they're only wanting your validation for what they've already done or decided to do: Tell me I'm right. This was different. Robert was authentically asking for advice.

"What did your mother say?"

"She doesn't talk to me much these days. Besides, I haven't told her yet."

"Don't." Sayles handed him the notebook. "It's nothing. Put it back in the box, Robert."

"Are you sure?"

"I'm sure. Back in the box and leave it there."

"Okay. Thank you, Detective." Robert replaced the notebook, pulled out the earphones and fingered them into his ears, pushed his cart on down the line.

Maybe ten words had passed between them all these years. So why had Robert picked him to talk to about this? To share what might be the only moral dilemma he'd ever—

Well, *that* was stupid. For all he knew, behind the apparent blandness, behind the dullness, Robert's every hour might be chockful of dilemmas, moral and otherwise. Things we all take for granted could be pitched battles—

And that was just as stupid from the other direction.

The closer you looked at the simplest thing, the deeper you dug, the more complicated it got. How could anyone ever fall folly to believing he understood *anything*?

Robert had parked his cart squarely by the wall, poured out dregs of coffee from both carafes, and begun rinsing them preparatory to making fresh.

Dolls.

And who *was* this guy? He'd had Lee Volheim, the department IT man he knew best, follow up on the e-mail. Bounced through half a dozen servers, Volheim said, commercial origin, a library, print shop, cybercafé. Like that. Best he could do.

*Doll Seller: We should meet*, Sayles had sent, suggesting an open, public place.

*No*, came the reply. He'd had to wait some time for it, as it bounced (he now knew) like a pinball from bumper to bumper.

*Where then?*

*Here.*

?

*On the Web.*

Right, Sayles thought. Here. Where you can remain a ghost.

Just after that, he and Graves had pulled a call, attempted murder. Turned out to be one of the expensive office complexes on Scottsdale Road near Biltmore Fashion Park, all copper-colored glass and reflected sunlight. Walked in on a man sitting at his desk and gone as pale as anyone Sayles'd ever seen. His right hand was pinned to the desk, teak from the look of it, with a letter opener shaped like a tiny samurai sword. His secretary, the swordsman, sat in a chair nearby, knees carefully together, hands on the chair arms, smiling.

# CHAPTER FIFTEEN

OKAY, SO HE'D SPENT most of the night throwing up, remains of his broiled fish and steamed vegetables swimming about the sink. He'd had to take his fingers and work the mess into the drain, water on full force the whole time. That didn't mean he was getting worse, getting closer. It could be these damn pills.

Sure it could. Or it could be the ozone layer. Or all the wastes, detergents, meds, and solvents leached into the water from the sewers and from there into the ground—like those wiping out whole species of birds and amphibians.

Sure.

Sunken eyes, hollows, shadow. Waxlike skin. The light coming from above the bathroom mirror in this Motel 8 or Paradise Motel or whatever the hell it was would make even a healthy, young man look ghostly. There were four bulbs set six inches apart. He held up his hand and turned: four dovetailed images on the wall. When he opened his hand, sixteen fingers moved all together. But not his blurred vision—not this time.

He came out of the bathroom as from a cave, blinking; past his window, daylight was kicking out its first footholds. He watched a bus disgorge its load of the last of the night folk heading home and replace them with those just beginning their day, wondering how many of them might be thinking about their lives, where they'd wound up, where they'd began, the curves and crooks and bland mystery of it all, all these Jonahs.

He had an hour before he was supposed to contact this cop, Sayles. Time enough for breakfast. And while his throat constricted at the thought of food, he needed to eat something, keep his strength up.

He had oatmeal at the cybercafé, eating slowly, and managed to keep it down. Sat there, because a blind man came in halfway through, seeing-eye dog curled beneath his table, remembering Witch.

Back in the day. He was renting this tiny house outside town, driving in for classes three days a week in a Dodge that, whenever it rained or got really humid, spewed smoke like a dragon. Ellie had moved in that August. Few months later she showed up—he and a paper on microeconomics were locked in a death struggle—with "a surprise for you," the surprise, out in her truck, being a sodden, swayback mutt of a dog she'd found advertised on the bulletin board at the Laundromat. Witch had immediately taken to him, would sit by his desk for hours as he studied, then get up and politely scratch at the door to go out. He'd watch her vanish into the high corn.

Then one afternoon she came back with blood on her muzzle, followed shortly by the landlord, Mr. Brenneman, who informed him that Witch had killed one of his sheep.

Christian apologized, and offered to pay, wondering how much a sheep might cost and where the hell he thought he'd get the money.

Mr. Brenneman didn't respond right away.

"Generally," he said, "we have to put them down, son. Once they get the taste for blood, they don't stop."

For better than a week, Christian kept Witch in, then one day, absorbed in schoolwork, without thinking about it when she scratched at the door, he got up and let her out. Sitting there peering hard into the latticework of quadratic equations, hoping that his vision somehow would clear, he heard the two shotgun blasts and knew instantly what they were. Hands poised above, he listened to the hum of his typewriter fill the new silence.

Within the month, Ellie was gone as well. And within the year, everything else of his life—as he sat enjungled, with undershirt, pants, a world-class case of athlete's foot, beer for breakfast, and no silence anywhere.

Finishing his oatmeal, Christian checked the clock again.

Time.

He had just signed on, moments later, when he heard a crash and someone saying, first softly, then loudly, "Joe? Joe?" Instantly, even after all these years, he was in go mode: battlefield breathing, eyes taking it all in, jamming the pieces together at some level below conscious thought. Man stood to get a refill, went down with mug in hand, took the table with him. Woman looking down, still sitting, round table rocking back and forth, dark stain (coffee? blood?) spreading on her skirt.

"Somebody . . . ?" she said.

And Christian was there, beside the man. Carotid pulse thready, skin pale and clammy, diaphoretic. Respirations shallow but regular.

"Sir, can you hear me?"

A nod.

"Open your eyes."

He did, and they darted about startled, so he'd definitely

been out. Pupils equal. And he tracked Christian's finger when asked.

"Ma'am, does he have heart problems that you know of?"

"I don't think so. He was just saying that he hadn't eaten all day."

Which probably meant that he hadn't drunk much of anything either. Christian was already dragging the chair over, propping the man's legs up on it.

Small infarction. Stroke. Or simply low blood sugar, hypotension.

As he rechecked the man's vitals, Christian could feel himself gearing down. But others had gathered around to watch, making him acutely aware that, in violation of years of discipline, he had made himself visible. Vulnerable.

"Do you know if he's diabetic?"

"I don't think so. I don't know. We just work together."

A young man, arms vivid with tattoos of imaginary beasts, had come out from behind the counter to ask if he could do anything.

"Probably only his blood sugar or blood pressure bottoming out, but it could be almost anything. Has someone called for paramedics?"

"On their way. We have to, whenever . . ." He pointed, apparently having used up all his words.

"Good." Slammed with sudden vertigo, right, left, up, and down gone missing from body and room—nothing to grab onto anywhere—Christian wasn't sure he could stand, or move at all. Thankfully, it was passing.

He looked at the clock. Unless the man was preternaturally patient, patience being altogether an unlikely virtue in a cop, he had missed his rendezvous with Sayles.

And he sure as hell had to be out of here before paramedics arrived and started asking questions.

# CHAPTER SIXTEEN

WHY IT HAD TO BE some specific time, fuck if he knew.

Just like he didn't have a clue what the hell good any of this could possibly do. But sure thing, let's get together at high noon and talk dolls. Why not. Be good for both of us.

So what *was* it about the time? A busy social life? Places to go, things to do? Simple control? "May be something to do with the bounces," Volheim had suggested, at Sayles's look quickly adding, "The routing? How he hops between servers?"

Sayles had just clicked on when the call came.

"Gonna need your help," Graves said at the other end.

"You still at court?"

"Well . . ."

Sayles watched the hour roll up on the counter. No idea if Dollman would wait. Or if, bottom line, he even cared.

"I'm in jail," Graves said.

"Sure you are."

"On contempt."

"You're a cop, for godsake. You were giving testimony."

"We drew Judge Lang. Just a step or two to the right of—hell, you know him. Getting ready to put Sidney away for the rest of his life when I politely asked for a word to the court. Damn, Sayles, the man was a fucking hero. I'm maybe two sentences in, when Lang says 'That will be enough.' 'No, it's not enough,' I said back, 'not nearly,' and I'm still saying my piece when his flunkies haul me out."

"He didn't just fine you?"

"Never went there. Sped right past, straight to lock-up."

"You must have hit a nerve—"

"Or he was already up in the tower looking for someone to shoot, yeah. You know how some of these shirts are. Puts on that damn robe, thinks he can do whatever the hell he wants in his courtroom."

Sad fact is, Sayles thought, he pretty much can.

"So where are you, Durango or Madison Street?"

"Madison."

"Overnight, I assume, since he was that pissed."

"Yeah, rest of the girls oughta be here soon for the sleepover."

"Okay, stay put."

"Funny."

"I'll go talk to the Cap. There's not much to be done at this point—you know that as well as I do. And you'll be out come morning, whatever."

Sayles hung up. Probably too late by now, but he logged on to the designated site anyway. Watched a discussion of snake handlers scroll steadily, line by line, down the screen, looking for the screen name Dollman said he'd be using. Hackneyed phrases passed through his mind: This cow don't give milk, Elvis has left the building, Lights are on and nobody's home.

Giving that up, he swung the cursor to Google *Hospice + Phoenix.* Over a hundred thousand hits. Adding *women* took it down to about thirty thousand. He clicked at random and read swatches of articles about the city's aging populace, baby boomers "easing" into their declining years, the exponential growth of extended-care facilities, family responsibility, community support. Many of the euphemisms had become as familiar to him and as oddly comforting as well-worn clothes. Declining years. Family ties. Waning faculties. Terminal care. Parades of word pairs that reminded him of comedy teams, one straight man earnest as the day is long, one innocent who just never quite gets it.

And he's been here, done this, how many times? Expecting what? To find something new? Suddenly to understand?

What was there to understand?

She was gone. Gone from his life, gone soon enough from her own.

He picked the new glasses up off his desk and put them on, aware as he did so of the world rushing toward him, fitting itself around him, taking him in. Better when the world's edges weren't so clear, he thought, when they're allowed to bleed, to run—that's where the interesting stuff happens.

So who was Dollman? And what was his interest in this? Chances that he had anything useful to offer were slim to none, of course. They'd had one brief Internet encounter before setting this up. Challenged, Dollman had provided details of the shooting—the attendants, what the victim had been wearing—but would go no further, proving only that he was present at the time. No proof at all that he wasn't just another one of the sick puppies that always came lapping around.

Sayles had picked at the doll thing till it went threadbare. Used up all his contacts, every resource person he knew inside and outside the department. Even called up a collector's shop out in Mesa and spent close to an hour hearing about porcelain, composition, cloth, vinyl, hard plastic, bisque, tin-head, and ball-joint dolls. Specialty furniture and clothes. Eyelashes, rooted hair, feather brows, pierced ears. Chicago's Doll Hospital, specializing in restorations of antiques. Dolly Lama out in Carslbad, chockful of ethnic and religious dolls. "Red Molly" Bing over in Utah with 4,673 dolls, so many that she bought a second house to put them in. There was a walkway . . .

Sayles had begged off at that point. Thanked him and hung up with the familiar sense of having touched, just beneath the surface of his own, another, previously unsuspected world.

Four thousand dolls. Never mind why, where did one *get* four thousand dolls?

Not a lot of specialty shops like his, the young-sounding man in Mesa had said, but a few. He could close the shop down tomorrow, in fact, and thrive on mail order. There was a sizable network of collectors forever buying and selling. Trading, too—quite a lot of that. Newsletters. Local and national conventions and such, loads of informal get-togethers. Web sites, many of them with forums.

Pushing up to the desk, Sayles thumped the mouse, watched Camelback and setting sun slide away. He clicked for Internet access, Googled *doll*, and hopscotched a dozen or so sites, winding up on eBay. Three or four of the descriptions sounded like close kin, he thought, similar phrasing, structure. Not too surprising, naturally, in such a niche market; formulas would develop, specific patterns of language emerge. "Item Location" listed one set of dolls (a family, no less) as being in Arizona, a Gilligan doll simply as "in the Great Southwest." Different screen names on all. He'd have to ask Volheim if there was some way of tracing them, tracking down the sellers' names and locations.

"You stag?"

He looked up. Will Stanford stood by the desk, tie stained with the remains of more than one meal but tugged into a perfect Windsor. Will pointed to the empty desk chair across from Sayles. "Flying solo, I mean. Or did Graves just finally get enough of you?"

Which reminded him that he needed to go talk to the captain.

Graves was thinking back to a response he'd been on when he was fresh on the streets. Some old guy called in a disturbance, his partner told him. Nine to one we get there and it's the kind who doesn't have a life, spends all his time worrying about what everybody else in the neighborhood is doing. They arrived to find a boy about eleven years old ushering an adult along the sidewalk toward a typical mid-city ranch house. The man looked to be early middle age, forty to fifty, wouldn't appear to need the help the boy was giving, but when you got close you saw something was wrong, something about the eyes and the way he moved. "He wanders," the boy told them, saying he needed to get him indoors if that was all right. Inside they found a woman somewhat older, sixties maybe, with another child, female, attending her. The home was spotlessly clean, everything in place. Doilies on tables, antimacassars on chairbacks, framed needlepoint homilies on the wall. *Love Binds Us, Bless This Our House.*

The kids were twins. Their father had been taking care of their mother up till a couple of years ago when he started getting sick too, at which point they had taken over care of both. Of course it was hard, they said when asked, looking surprised—surprised not at the question, but that the two policemen would think there was anything strange about their assuming care.

Graves remembered the kids' names, Alexander and Isobel.

A lot of responds followed that one, he was new, shifts were packed with challenge, danger, new experiences, apprehension. So he never followed up, never found out what became of the family, what had been wrong with the older Glaisters. Never even thought much about it till years later, and when he did, he got to wondering if it might be something hereditary, something the kids had in them too.

Probably best not to think about that, take that too far.

Given where he was right now, probably best not to think too hard about much of anything.

# CHAPTER SEVENTEEN

THE BOY CAN COOK.

He didn't know why, but the phrase, a remark his father had made years ago, always went through his mind when he was in the kitchen, rolled around and around in there like a loose ball bearing. He'd learned in pure self-defense, unable to digest, barely even to eat, what his mother put on the table those times she tried at all, but he'd come to like it. It made sense to him. Once you got the basic moves down, broiling, braising, browning, roasting, you pretty much had it. Reliable commonality in combinations of flavors, spices, and sauces, all built up from sweet, sour, savory, salty. You started with one thing, added others, turned it all into something else. Cooking made sense the way geometry or numbers made sense.

He had put on stew meat earlier, fire as low as he could get it and as little water as he could get away with, and was chopping celery, onions, carrots, and potatoes to add.

Cooking made sense. The dreams were another matter.

This time he had been walking down a long corridor. People

watched from within the frosted-glass doors that lined either side. He couldn't make out features, couldn't see the heads really—just ill-defined ovoids that changed shape behind the glass as they went from profile to straight to profile, tracking his progress. There were small numbers on the upper left-hand corner of the doors' glass panels, like page numbers in a book: 231, 230, 229. And a window far ahead at corridor's end, black beyond. As he passed door after door, though he still couldn't really see them, the heads appeared to change more substantially, becoming larger, out of proportion, like the heads of animals.

He never felt the pain, just looked down to see blood spreading over the cutting board, chopped onions gone pink. Even then, it didn't register. He stood holding the knife in his right hand, thumb and middle finger still around the onion, tip of his index finger lying alongside. Interesting how, instead of blossoming into pain, the finger went numb, as though it were not even there, as though it were someone else's finger. It bent when he willed it, but he couldn't feel the movement.

In the bathroom he ran cold water over the oozing raw flesh, poured peroxide over it, held a compress against it. Feeling slowly returned, first as pins and needles, then as burning pain. He'd dealt with injuries before, even closed a three-inch slice in his arm with butterflies improvised from adhesive tape, but he couldn't think how he might be able to fix this. Supergluing the tip back on didn't seem like a good idea.

Mrs. Flores opened her door wearing an apron and a surprised expression. Her eyes went directly from his face to his hand. The washcloth he'd wrapped around his finger was dark with blood.

Ten minutes later he was in her friend's truck, a comfortably middle-aged Ford F-150 that had at least three different colors of paint warring across hood, fenders, and bed, being driven to a free clinic that, Mrs. Flores said, wouldn't ask questions. She still had her apron on.

Three hours after that, he was sitting at the table in her house having dinner with Mrs. Flores, her friend Felix, and two neighborhood kids of eleven or twelve who seemed simply to have wandered into the house in time to eat. Platters of *machaca* and of sizzling pepper and onions moved steadily around the table. Mrs. Flores heated tortillas on the open burner of her stove, dropping them on, turning, serving.

His finger throbbed now. A big-nosed doctor had cleaned and bandaged it tightly. Very clean, he said. You may lose some feeling in that finger, but it's going to be fine. We'll give you a shot, antibiotics, just to be on the safe side. He looked at Mrs. Flores. Bring the boy back if he starts running a fever, sweating, drinking a lot, anything like that.

*The boy.*

Felix pushed the *machaca* toward him. "How'd you cut yourself?"

"Not paying attention."

"How accidents mostly happen."

Jimmie didn't have much by way of social conversation but gave it a shot. "What do you do, Mr. . . . ?"

"Just Felix. Nobody calls me anything but Felix." He exchanged glances with Mrs. Flores. "Drive trucks, mostly."

"He helps people," Mrs. Flores said.

"Like he did me, today."

"It was nothing," Felix said, then, smiling at Mrs. Flores: "Es nada."

"I'm going to be a football player," one of the kids said.

"And I'm going to own my own business," the other said.

Jimmie asked him what kind of business.

"Don' know. Big one."

It was getting dark outside, trees going gray, fading into the grayness around them. Everyone said this used to be pure desert, then people moved in from elsewhere and brought along their trees and bushes and backyards. But everyone also said there used to be rivers here, and boats going down them, so go figure.

"I should be getting home," Jimmie said. "Can I help clean up?"

"We can help, Mama Flores," one of the kids said.

"Looks like we have it covered, then." Mrs. Flores leaned close to him as she scooped dishes from the table. "Are you going to be okay?"

Jimmie stood, and nodded. "Thank you both, more than I can say." He held out his hand, and Felix, looking a little surprised, shook it. They walked together into the front room. When Felix switched on the porch light and opened the door, a moth flew in. Without apparent effort or thought, Felix lifted his hand, intercepted the moth, carried it outside with them.

"Roshelle wants me to tell you," he said, "you need anything, you just come right on back here."

"I will. And thanks again."

Felix let the moth go. "A pleasure," he said.

Back at the house, Jimmie cleaned up the kitchen as best he could with one hand pretty much out of commission. The finger was thickly bandaged. The big-nosed doctor had cautioned him against getting the dressings wet. He felt every heartbeat there at the fingertip, like those cartoons where thumbs or heads blow up like balloons, deflate, and blow up again. He put the pot with the stew meat in the refrigerator, tossed the vegetables. He'd start fresh tomorrow.

Flipping the computer on, he thought about Mrs. Flores, Felix, and the kids, this ramshackle, sort-of family of hers, as it booted up. He thought of the moth Felix had taken outside, and remembered his mother proudly showing him her mason jar of mosquitoes.

Once when he was small, they'd been out walking and come across a pigeon with a broken wing. It must have just happened, he realized now, thinking about it. The bird would walk a few steps, then hop, trying to fly, as the wing just hung there, fanned out, at its side. The bird couldn't understand: this had always worked. It took three steps, hopped again, fluttering the good wing. Jimmie looked over and saw tears on his mother's face.

Now, remembering that, what came to him was the thought of how panicked the bird must have been, how lost, how the only thing it could do was keep trying.

He entered his password, travelR2, to check on orders. Four of them, including the set of luthier tools he'd figured to be a tough sell. He'd bought the set from the family of a Filipino ukulele maker; it came wrapped in goatskin, which was how, the family said, he always kept them. Jimmie acknowledged the orders, promised shipping first thing tomorrow, then e-mailed for package pickup. Business as usual. Not a big business, but his.

He logged on to check payments, then began his cruise of sites where he regularly picked up items for resale. Over time he had found his way to some fairly obscure sites. These didn't take long, as turnover was slow, and often a glance was enough before moving on. Even with the common sites, eBay and so on, one learned to scan efficiently: using keywords, selecting chronological entries, and skipping to the end, setting very specific search parameters.

His eyes went down the pages:

Printing press circa 1919, fully functional
Loom, brought over from Scotland
Artist action mannikin, 15 inch
Planter made from authentic coolie hat
Button collection, over 1,000!

He read the entries, registered them as his eyes moved down the listings. He flagged four to keep watch on. But he wasn't there, not really. He was walking down that corridor again, watching the featureless heads turn toward him. He was beside his mother on the street, watching the pigeon try to fly.

# CHAPTER EIGHTEEN

"THING ABOUT IT IS, you sit there and you're mad, but after a while the mad starts to get boring, so you move on, think about other stuff. How often do you get the chance, day to day, to just sit and think?"

*Too often.*

"And you for damn sure can't sleep. Sounds like a train station down in there. Doors clanging, walls shaking, voices everywhere. Footsteps you hear from half a mile away. Deep thoughts, that's what come to you. What's it all about, why are we here, who am I. All that shit. Then you look around and all at once you see it's like you're back in college, this steaming mass of bodies, bullshit, attitude, big talk."

Having never been to college, Sayles wouldn't know. Back in the day, when he came on the job, high school was good enough; lot of old-timers didn't have that. Nowadays, newbies like Graves, they knew everything. Stop for hot dogs at a roach coach and you'd hear about the industrial revolution. By the time your indigestion kicked in some miles down the road, they'd be on to union activity in the forties, maybe hum a bar or two of "Which Side Are You On?"

Truth to tell, Sayles often thought of his partner as pompous and full of himself, never far away from cutting one fine figure of fool. Kind of guy who grew up in Cedar Rapids on meat loaf and green bean casserole and just *knew* he was beyond all that. But Sayles also had to remember how many times he'd seen Graves turn on a dime, veering from his usual mode to sudden, wheels-down compassion in the presence of real pain.

Graves waved a hand. "And then I woke up." He waited. "It's the punch line—"

"I know, Graves. I know. But what the hell are you doing here? You just got out, right? Why aren't you home? Showering, sleeping, having a stiff one?"

"And pass up all this?" He cast a glance, proud shepherd, out over the field of desks, chairs, side tables, and filing cabinets. "I would not, however, pass up a kind offer of breakfast."

At the Early Bird, surrounded by lawyers prepping clients or puffing out cheeks at one another, businessmen with laptops, and slow-eyed hospital workers going off shift, Sayles heard about his partner's prison experience, which sadly, unlike what people seemed to claim these days of just about anything from reading a bestseller to going to the dentist, had not changed his life.

As they ate, Sayles brought Graves up to speed on their cases, not that there was much speed to any of them. Janice Beck's boyfriend had come in to confess, saying he put her and the child in the cedar chest to keep them "fresh" and keep the bugs away. They'd packed him off to the psych ward. The Navajo girl from the irrigation ditch, that one was starting to look not random like they first thought, or gang related, but like the stepmother's doing; she'd had a hand in the pot, anyway. When Sayles came to

Rankin's shooting, he didn't mention the doll connection, the note left for him at his home, or his Internet communications with an apparent witness.

"Something'll turn up," Graves said.

"Sure it will." Tomorrow's a new day and all that.

Two tables over, a man sat feeding the froth off his latte to his three-year-old, skimming it up half a spoonful at a time. Two servers, one male, one female, stood in the entryway by the kitchen door talking about a concert they'd been to. A woman walked out of the dress shop across the street with a single elegantly wrapped package.

All around him, people were going on with their lives, things pretty much the same day to day. Mothers were dying, husbands slipping away, new wars breaking out and old ones from years before continuing, but their lives went right on. Certainly not the first time he'd had the thought. Just seemed he was having it more and more often of late.

Then, and with no idea why he was doing this, Sayles leaned in close over the table and told Graves about Josie: how he'd got up and found her gone, the medications she'd ditched, the note, where she was.

Getting Graves home took some time. Road crews were tearing up Central again, and every alternate Sayles tried, Seventh, Osborn, turned out to be as hopeless. They sat through change after change of light at Indian School watching the light rail glide by. Sayles's revelation had visibly subdued him, but his partner was wired. Nerves, adrenaline, sleeplessness. Residual anger. Sayles had told Graves how he sat outside the hospice some nights.

"And you don't go in?"

Sayles shook his head.

"Why?"

Respect. Honor. Fear.

But how, not why, was the true question. *How* could he do that, not go inside, see her? Over and again we manage to convince ourselves that we're doing what's right, even when our actions violate another's wishes, the will of society itself, and all good sense. It would be so easy for him to say, Josie really does want me there, or to decide that it had to be, after all, in her best interest. But a quieter voice always surfaced. Well, not so much surfaced as made its presence known. Like that unease that settles on you and you don't know where it comes from.

Still a lot of day left when he got back to the squad. He paged through the five case folders on top. Sometimes something will jump out at you. Or something will seep in, do its work later, cause you to look at what's on the table in a different way. One of his high school teachers had a favorite saying: You gotta take time to shake the jar.

So he shook and shook, and not much happened.

Late that afternoon he fielded a call to a Circle K where "some old dude was hanging around outside hassling customers" and it looked like there might be a body back in the alley. Patrol car called in asking for a supervisor or detective. Man was all of forty, possibly a deaf-mute, possibly just too addled to speak intelligibly. The body was the man's ragged bedroll. Sayles gave him five dollars.

# CHAPTER NINETEEN

FROM ACROSS THE STREET he watched John Rankin hobble out the side door by the carport and stand in his robe and bare feet. The man had survived the gunshot, would have recovered in short order, but the cardiac arrest had drained him, tapped his body out. You could see the exhaustion in his walk, defeat in the slump of his body. Even at this remove, his skin looked gray. So they'd brought him around, but the heart had been damaged. And once the heart stopped, other organs started sliding south, so he probably had further damage, could be easing into kidney failure. Maybe even a touch of brain dysfunction, to judge by the slight drag of his left foot. A light stroke—or anoxia.

We spend as little time as possible dwelling on the shambles we're likely to become, and for good reason. TV, movies, they save the guy's life, the last you see of him he's getting rolled out of the hospital in a bright chrome wheelchair. Never mind that he can't feed himself, that his constant drool is so nasty it eats through his shirts, or that he pees himself constantly in little geysers that smell of rot.

Strange neighborhood out here, five minutes from the city, felt more like small town than suburb. Homes with sagging roofs and vehicles parked in the yard abutted others with manicured lawns and monogrammed shutters. One family up the street apparently lived in a front yard packed with chairs, an old couch, children's wading pools and toys, a table or two, multiple coolers. Walking by another, he wondered when he'd last seen window boxes with flowers in them.

Two days, and no sign of the wife. Social worker of some kind, he remembered. Maybe his information was wrong and they'd split up before this. Or maybe she couldn't handle what happened, packed it in and walked. Single car, the year-old Hyundai that stayed in the carport. Rankin would come out, pick up the newspaper or look around, go in. Once he came back out right away and half-pulled, half-pushed the recycle bin to curbside. The bench under the picture window in front of the house was thick with spiderwebs. Rankin turned the TV on when he got up in the morning, turned it off when he went to bed for the night. Light flickered against the drapes, and as dark fell you could watch the screen through them.

Okay, so he *wasn't* going to let it go.

Not that he had much idea what he was doing here, what he expected. Just he was paying attention, looking as always for the thing that didn't fit.

Far as he could tell, the cop, Sayles, was out of the picture. He hadn't expected much to come of that anyway, but hey, good for a try. Hadn't found out anything more from him and didn't look like he would. That left Rankin himself.

Christian had been watching for the better part of four days. If the guy's life was nondescript before, now it had gone positively featureless. No visitors. No activity. No clothes other than T-shirt, boxers, and bathrobe, as far as he had seen. The TV went on, the TV went off. Lights did the same: living room, back bedroom, bathroom, kitchen. Simple points against which to graph a man's life.

Of course, it wasn't Rankin that he was watching.

The rental car smelled of stale fried food with an overlay of pine scent from someone's misguided attempt to fix that. He'd looked at five or six before taking it. The others were spiff and clean and newish. This one wasn't. He'd been out to check the neighborhood, knew what would fit in, what was likely to be noticed. He had a thermos of coffee, two sandwiches from a mom-and-pop convenience store, chocolate, an apple. A newspaper he could pretend to be reading should he draw anyone's attention.

He was thinking how kids back in school, kids these days too, he was sure, always talked about being bored, and how he could never understand that. The way wind moved in the trees, the sheen of sunlight on glass or steel, a fly's wings—everything was of interest. You just had to pay attention, you just had to *look*.

Reaching to roll down the window, he saw that his hand shook and swallowed one of the pills, followed it with coffee.

Evidence of kids everywhere here. The wading pools in the inside-out living room up the street, swing sets jutting above fences in backyards, bicycles in driveways, posters in windows.

Mr. Earll lived down the street from them when Christian was a kid. He was old, much older than the wife with whom he'd had two children. Old enough to be her father, everyone said, then paused before adding *or worse*. From Christian's earliest memories, Mr. Earll had lived not in the house but in the garage around back, going in only for meals. Like he'd served his purpose and wasn't of use anymore. Been a bachelor all his life and couldn't get used to anything else, the kinder souls among them said. Had a TV out there, on which he watched all the comedies, Andy Griffith, Lucy, Danny Thomas, and never laughed. Maybe he went inside to sleep; Christian wondered. But he was always out there, and the TV was always on. Mr. Earll had been a teacher, taught science at the local high school for better than forty years. Yeah, the kids said, he's so old he was around when they *invented* science.

Christian went to school with the younger brother, Jerry Earll, who acted like everything was perfectly normal back at the house. Hell, for him, it *was* normal. That age, we think whatever we see around us, that's what there is. The old man died their junior year. His wife found him out there early one morning sitting in his ratty old recliner, TV on, nothing but a test pattern and static.

Christian's eyes went to the tan Honda even before it turned into the street. He'd seen it, or one just like it, earlier today. Stock and boxy, three to five years old, no parking decals, bumper stickers, or other markers, local plate, tires good but had some miles on them. Single occupant. The Honda swung easily, unhurriedly, around the corner at Cumberland, headed his way. Christian picked up the newspaper.

Probably a neighborhood car, cutting through, cruising home. But as it reached Rankin's house, he was sure the driver's head turned that way, and turned back only after it was past. Then it was abreast of the rental. Three dents in the front fender spaced like on a pawn shop sign—so it *was* the car he'd seen earlier. Just as Christian lowered the newspaper, the driver looked his way.

Christian knew that face . . .

Suddenly dizzy, he put his head back on the seat. There was a moment when he felt the world spiraling down around him, contracting. Then nothing.

His left arm wouldn't move.

His eyes opened to bright, bright lights. Water-stained tile ceiling. Faces. Then, in a rush, sounds.

"He's coming up."

"Sir, you're all right, can you hear me?"

"I'm seeing redness and swelling by the IV site, Doctor."

"Infiltrated?"

"Line's patent. Reaction?"

"You're in the hospital, sir. You passed out."

"Ambye."

"What?"

"Otics."

Someone leaned close. Coffee on her breath.

It was the antibiotics. For years never had a problem. Then, last time, his skin turned so red it looked like he'd been boiled, and hives the size of marbles broke out everywhere. Armpits, groin, even (he'd swear) inside his eyelids.

"No sign of anaphylaxis."

"Resp's steady at fourteen, sat ninety-four, BS good bilaterally."

Christian lifted his head. The arm was strapped down, with two IVs running piggyback. He tried again:

"Antibiotics."

"You're allergic?" Lilt to the soft voice, an accent. Nigerian, maybe.

He nodded, remembering how the young resident had insisted that he was not allergic, merely sensitive, to the cephalosporin he'd been given. Still a little goofy from sedation, he'd drifted off thinking how he was now a sensitive male. When he woke again, thanks to steroids, the hives were gone.

"Can you tell us your name, sir?" Duh-duh-DA-duh-duh-DA-duh.

This time, too, he was still a little goofy. He tried to remember what name was on the ID he'd been carrying and couldn't.

"Christian," he finally said.

"I'm sorry, are you asking for a minister, sir?"

"Christian. My name." All these years, even when he thought of himself that way, he'd never used the name. "What everyone calls me."

"Oh, I see. And how are you, Christian?"

"Okay."

"Can you tell us what happened?"

He shook his head.

"Are you diabetic?"

"No."

"Have you a history of heart problems? Seizures?"

"No."

"The EMTs brought in meds. These were in the automobile with you. You were taking these?"

"Yes."

"One is prescription, a common pain medication, quite strong. The other, we cannot identify."

Belgium. He'd flown there from Paris. A ground-floor flat on the waterfront that looked more like a library or professor's study than a physician's office. He remembered bright red and yellow flowers on tall stems in a vase at the window. Dr. Van Veeteren had a poorly repaired harelip. He smelled of rosewater and stale cigarette smoke.

"Lab work's in, Doctor."

The woman above him turned away, turned back holding a sheet of printout paper. He watched her eyes move down it, then shift to him. She said nothing, but the question was in her eyes.

"Yes," he said. "I know."

# CHAPTER TWENTY

WHEN HE WOKE, he couldn't feel his hand. Then he lifted it, into a faint burr of light from the window, and the pain started up. Not pain, really, more a simple insistence: rock in your shoe, the tooth you keep probing with your tongue. Blood had seeped into the bandage, turning it hard and crusty. It crackled when he pushed at it. There'll be some leakage, the big-nosed doctor told him, blood, interstitial fluids—and scarring. But we'll have to wait to see how much of that.

He had no idea what time it was. Dark, and he had slept, slept hard from the feel of it. For a moment when he first woke, he was disoriented, adrift, unsure where he was. Then the familiar sounds and light, the familiar smells, came to him.

Home.

Through the drapes (his mother, he remembered, always called them drapes, never curtains) he could see the moon, low in the sky, but he wasn't really sure what that meant. Early in the night? Late?

She'd wanted to leave them open, believing that the strained, pale light from outside would comfort him. He'd asked her, many times, not to, and she said Okay, I understand, you're a big boy now, but she always forgot. Once she was gone, he would close them.

He got up and switched the computer on, typing awkwardly. With the three good fingers of his left hand, and the bandaged one in the way however he held it, it was like a man walking with a clubfoot or with one leg shorter than the other, limping and pitching. He checked mail, then ran his usual sites, rifling through them automatically, Downer Loads, The Great Illusion, The Real Triangle, Traveler. He watched the screen, and at some level he was reading, but his thoughts were elsewhere.

The comfort his mother had thought he might take from that light, he found in the dark. He loved the way the dark closed around him, held him. Everything slowing, slowly growing still and quiet. He relished, thrilled at, put off for as long as possible the moment he would reach to turn off the light. Mystery, incalculable freedom, and safety all swaddled together in that moment, in that other, wholly private world opening to him.

But also, of late, the dreams.

Opening his eyes, he had not known where he was. A bright room, movement all around him. Woman's face above his. Her lips were moving but there was no sound. No sound anywhere, though people walked past, doors open and shut, carts and equipment wheeled by. He lifted his head, looked down at the arm strapped in place, paper tape over needles and puffy skin. His feet, splayed in a lazy V, looked like they were a mile away. He was nude, only a towel draped over his midsection. And more than sound was missing: he couldn't feel his body.

But of course it wasn't his body.

There was a blank then, white space in the dream or in his memory of the dream, he didn't know which, and when it clicked back in, he was making his way down a stairway. He'd got clothes somewhere, too small but wearable, and blood ran down his arm where the tape and needles had been. The lights out here were harsh, stark. A sign on the door at the bottom of the stairs read

EMERGENCY EXIT
AN ALARM WILL SOUND

and he stood there a moment in indecision. A man and woman came out onto the landing above, talking loudly, and paused before continuing upward. Their feet rang on the steel stairs.

He looked down at the body supporting him. This was the opposite of the comfort to be found in darkness. He was in a strange place, unsure of himself and surroundings, exposed, vulnerable . . .

*Who* was exposed and vulnerable?

Jimmie tried to remember if he had ever before dreamed as someone else. Others in dreams changed, sure, the walk-ons, the companions, but weren't people always themselves in their dreams?

No sense in putting this off. Whatever he was doing, he'd best be about it.

Choose.

Act.

The door had one of those lever bars on it. He touched it, ready to push, steeling himself for the alarm. The bandage was there, hard and crusty, on the hand at the end of someone else's arm.

# CHAPTER TWENTY-ONE

WHAT HE COULDN'T GET OVER, was his sense of violation.

The hallway was long and without windows, painted bright yellow in an attempt to counter the dimness and shut-in feel. Free-form paintings running low on the walls had been done by children from the local school, she'd told him. Lots of fat-bodied animals with stick-figure legs.

"I'm afraid I may have called you for nothing," she said now. "And overstepped. Seriously overstepped?" She reached reflexively to push back her hair; either the close-cropped style was recent, or it was a habit she couldn't shake. Her name tag read *Ms. Zelazny, RN*. She'd introduced herself on the phone as Judy. "I took it upon myself . . ." Her hand barely grazed his shoulder. "I am *so* sorry."

"The important thing is, she's better now."

"Out of danger, as they say, yes. For the time being."

"As they also say." He looked in through the glass portion of the door. "What happened?"

"She stopped breathing. Her blood pressure bottomed out.

Usually . . . You know that she refuses all medication? Accepts only basic care?"

He nodded. Now he knew.

"Once in a great while she'll ask for a Tylenol. I think . . . I shouldn't be saying this, but I think the pain just got to be too much for her. She gave up—just for a moment."

The nurse was quiet then, giving him time. He could hear her breathing there beside him, almost feel the warmth of her skin.

"She said she didn't want to fight this. In the note she left me. That it wasn't in me to understand."

"We don't know what's in us, do we? We think we do. Then . . ."

Sayles had conducted thousands of interviews. He knew when an explanation was coming. You could see the story starting up in their eyes, the shift in body balance, a certain charge in the air.

"My mother, my biological mother, died in a prison hospital. She was alone, surrounded by people she didn't know, had no family to speak of. I've always wondered what she might have been thinking, there at the end. No one should . . ."

Elevator doors opened and a food cart rolled off. It made a terrible clatter and smelled of gravy.

"I shouldn't have called, I'm sorry. It was not my place."

"I'm glad you did. Thank you." He looked back into the room. An aide was repositioning Josie on her side, tucking pillows behind and around. "It would be better if she doesn't know I was here."

"Yes. Yes, I suppose it might. If there's anything . . ."

He smiled and started back down the hall, wondering what Judy Zelazny's incomplete sentences, her trailings off, said about who she was, her connection to the world.

Outside, he watched a couple of dust devils skip and spin about the parking lot, then got in the car. He sat there a while, his thoughts skittering to and fro like the dust devils and every bit as insubstantial, nervous movement with no purpose, no purchase.

The moon hung high over Camelback, full and orange. Against scattered clouds he could see smoke gathering from a fire off to the west, industrial by the look of it, out by the White Tanks, maybe.

He got home with no memory of starting the car, or of the drive. Hung his sport coat on one of the hooks inside the kitchen door, pulled a beer from the refrigerator, and thumbed on the computer, thinking to read the news. Mostly he stayed off the computer at home, got enough of that on the job, but he'd canceled the newspaper months ago—they kept piling up outside, unretrieved—and was seriously in arrears with the world and its goings-on. Plus, he didn't want to think. Not tonight.

But it wasn't to be. In turn he attempted to focus on war news, financial news, political news, and sports news, and failed with each pass. Even the op-eds and columns seemed incomprehensible. As though it were all taking place in some land far removed from his own.

He had put the new glasses on and taken them off again repeatedly while surfing. Every time he got new ones, he went through a period when he was certain they'd done the prescription wrong, but this was worse than usual. He simply couldn't or wouldn't keep the damned things on. Stubbornness? Since, when it came right down to it, he saw fine with them.

He grabbed a second beer, went into the front room, and turned on the TV. His last possible refuge—but with the first light from the screen, memories of Josie, of her TV forever on, forever whispering, slammed into him. He clicked through channel after channel barely seeing what was before him, a Victor

Mature movie, reruns of Kojak, religious programming, Hispanic stations, long-winded ads for exercise equipment, knife sets, and revolutionary cleaning supplies, before coming to rest at KAET. A nature show about, of all things, the mating patterns of insects. He sat watching, thinking vaguely that this world, the insect world, seemed to him no more alien than one in which people tried to sell memorial plates to insomniacs and day sleepers at three A.M.

The show about insects gave way to one about birds, and he remembered a story that had been passing around the station for years. Apocryphal, for all he knew, but the older cops swore by it. Happened way back, they said. This guy, just someone off the street, no one the family knew or anything like that, had killed a man and his wife and two kids in their beds. So next he goes into the kitchen and makes himself a sandwich. Eats it and puts on coffee. And while the coffee's brewing, he goes through the house methodically killing the family pets. Scoops fish out of the tank and throws them on the floor, steps on them. Slits the dog's throat with a chef's knife from the kitchen. Strangles the parakeet. Next week, on a call from a neighbor, they find him in another house. Man and his son are dead, he's in the kitchen eating a bowl of Cheerios. Hasn't got to the dog or cat yet.

Sayles thought about how so many stories come down to good and evil, guy in the white hat and guy in the black, hawk and dove, this struggle between them, like one will win. You saw and read and heard that long enough, you started to believe it, started to think like that. But the bad stuff is right there with you, always. It's the friend you're walking down the street with, you're both talking away, then he turns and there's something different in his eyes, or in yours. And you both go quiet.

Sayles switched the TV off and sat listening to the sounds of the house around him, familiar sounds, comforting sounds, waiting for light to start up. It was out there somewhere in the night, feeling its way blindly toward him.

# CHAPTER TWENTY-TWO

FIRST THING HE HAD TO DO was get to an ATM, buy some decent clothes that fit and would allow him to blend in. Lucky his shoes had made it to the room with him, at least. None of his clothes had. He'd grabbed pants and a shirt from the room next to his, single bed with an old man who watched his every move and never made a sound. He'd already pulled back the inner soles of his shoes to check on the bank cards stashed there for emergencies. But this too-small polyester shirt and these orangish slacks with trampled cuffs wouldn't do.

They'd rolled him up to a room, finally, stretcher piloted by a young Asian man who wheeled at what seemed double speed through halls and doorways, avoiding crash after crash by scant millimeters. Hot on their trail came Miss Feyn from Admissions. It was imperative that she get information. Each time she asked his name, Social Security number, home address, insurance carrier, he would begin to answer, then nod off. The drugs they'd given him, of course. She shuffled her papers and feet, looked out the window, and finally said, I'll have to come back later.

Filling the space Miss Feyn left appeared a nurse who never

gave her name, welcomed him to the unit, and explained that, if there was nothing he needed at the moment, they were getting ready for shift change and someone would be with him shortly to get him checked in and settled.

So he waited. Heard elevator doors open and close, loud greetings, laughter, banter. In a few minutes that subsided, and he knew they were in report, one or two left behind at the nurse's station to keep watch, the rest in seclusion.

He rolled his legs over the side of the bed and sat for moments as the room stopped pitching and weaving, then experimentally stood. Not too unsteadily—and not bad, considering all that had gone down. Ripping off the tape, he pulled the IVs one by one, pushed and held his thumb against each site to minimize bleeding. His blood ran thin; minor cuts would bleed and bleed.

That done, he slipped on his shoes and went next door to borrow clothing from his neighbor.

As he walked past the nurse's station, the woman sitting there looked up. He smiled, thanked her, and added that he'd be back for the next visiting hours.

The alarm hadn't sounded when he went out the door, but the heat had slammed into him, left him shaken, breathless. He walked slowly, clamping down with his will, deep breath, hold, exhale, and soon enough was a fair imitation of normal. Four blocks along, he found a Circle K.

There were two ahead of him. An Hispanic man in his early twenties repeatedly reinserted his card as he leafed through the growing collection of transaction slips. An older woman, wearing what these days they called business casual, waited behind him; with each new try she rolled her eyes. When at last the young man gave up and her turn came, she counted her money, recounted it, placed the bills precisely in her pocketbook, filed away the transaction slip with what looked to be a year's worth of them, then painstakingly fitted her bank card back into the foremost photo sleeve. At the counter she bought a bottled water and a lottery ticket.

Two hours later, scrubbed and still wet, with the air conditioner vent blowing up at him, he stood at the window of the Tropicana Motel, whose palm-tree sign, pool, and desk clerk had all seen better days, though probably not a hell of a lot better. The pool bore a layer of leaves and mostly dead insects that in fact looked much like the desk clerk's skin. Foot-high weeds grew from cracks in the parking lot. Many of the doors he passed on the way to his room showed signs of having been in the past forcibly sprung.

In an adjoining room a TV played. There was something wrong with the TV, or with the reception, so that the sound was mostly static, but no one seemed to care. Maybe they'd gone out, or checked out, and left it on. But he'd heard the toilet flush over there a while back.

The bleeding had stopped, the dizziness hadn't. And he didn't have his pills. Everything else was replaceable. The pills weren't. But then . . . maybe that was just as well. He held up his hand and willed the tremor to stop. It did—or he persuaded himself that it had. And why would it matter which was true?

No pills. What he *did* have was a drive he hadn't known for a long time now, muscle, a purpose behind his actions: finding who had attacked John Rankin. *Why* he was doing it remained opaque, impenetrable. Not pride. Not honor. Certainly not a sense of justice. But there it was, the road before him. And finally the why didn't matter any more than the truth of whether or not his tremors had actually stopped.

In early youth he'd read a lot of fiction. Novels like *Treasure Island* and the Tom Swift books, short stories published by the dozen in magazines back then, *Redbook*, *Argosy*, *Boy's Life*. Over time it came to him that most fiction, maybe all of it, from the grandest tales to the most commonplace, was about things that were missing. Family, lovers, sustenance, peace, ideals. At the heart of all those stories were emptinesses, yearnings, hollows that couldn't be filled—as though bereavement were hardwired into mankind.

And that was a thing he never felt, could not understand. Like music.

It was then he knew that he was different. Apart somehow, exempt. Not different in the way every adolescent feels, but substantially, deeply, definitively different, in ways that couldn't be breached.

And now, comically, he seemed to have his answer to a question he had felt no need to ask. Finding his usurper, finding Rankin's attacker. A passion, a purpose.

Back in Rankin's hospital room he had stood, pretending to note something on his clipboard, something about the lines supplying medical gases, as he tracked approaching footsteps. Turned to confront a man in gray suit, blue shirt. A man with strong hands who seemed out of place, who didn't quite fit. A cop or hospital official, he had thought at the time, though neither seemed likely.

Then, before he woke up in the hospital himself, the driver of a tan Honda with three dents in the front fender, cruising by Rankin's house a second time. And the face turning toward him the same as the one back in Rankin's hospital room.

He was sure of it.

That night in his sleep he took his place in a long line of people moving slowly forward, inch by inch, hundreds of them, people as far as he could see, people ahead of him, people behind. No one knew where they were going. No one left the line. They continued to move forward. Slowly. By inches. Beneath a sky neither dark nor light.

# CHAPTER TWENTY-THREE

GRAVES ALWAYS THOUGHT of himself as a private man. Always tried to respect the privacy of others.

This thing with Sayles, though. With Josie, her there in the what-do-you-call-it, the hospice, and him not going to see her. Sitting out front of the place like some damn teenager or stalker. Hard not to say something.

He'd been thinking about it ever since Sayles dropped him off at his house.

He was sitting in his favorite spot, the glider on the back porch, looking out on oleanders that cut the yard off from all else, holding a beer that he kept forgetting to drink. The oleanders were tugging at the phone lines again. He'd have to take care of that soon. But he'd bought the house for the oleanders as much as for anything else. Walked right through the house onto the back porch and said he'd take it. Never had a house before. Even back when Jennie was around, they'd rented. They talked about freedom a lot back then.

Freedom.

Big words, big ideas. Fit okay when you were young. And it

wasn't that you outgrew them, it was just that after a while you started looking silly wearing them.

Back then, you'd have had a hard time picking anyone less likely to become a cop. He'd been in grad school, studying history. And Jennie was making perfumes, candles, what she called essences, selling them at art fairs and gift shops, then got into Internet sales early on. Jennie was rich now, living in Mexico, some kind of artist's colony. He heard from her every month or so by e-mail.

Hell, even he had trouble reconstructing how it happened. They ran out of money, of course. So much for the MA. He taught as a sub, mostly elementary school, which he hated, then a procession of I'm-not-really-just-a-worker jobs: bookstore sales, editing a trade publication, project manager at a credit card company. Fielded calls at a suicide prevention center for a time. Ended up clerking in a law office where police frequently came to be deposed or coached prior to testimony. He'd talk to them on breaks, hang with them as they waited their turn.

Shazam.

Before he knows it he's sitting in a patrol car that stinks of feet and fast food and gasoline fumes watching a kid that's not more than twelve years old run out of a mom-and-pop store carrying a gun big as his head.

He understands his limits, never had pretentions to being a great cop. He does the job. He thinks and acts in straight lines. He's smarter than most, and quick, so he did well as a line officer, moved up the line at a steady pace.

Years back, he'd taken one of those left brain/right brain tests. A woman in silhouette spinning endlessly. If you saw the spin as counterclockwise, it meant the left brain, the logical part, was dominant. Clockwise, the right brain, the creative side, was dominant. That woman had never spun other than counterclockwise for him, and never would.

Unlike Sayles, he's predictable. Same procedures, same moves, again and again. No sudden connections, none of those damned patterns Sayles was always talking about, just A to B to C; he goes off to the side, he loses it.

Sayles probably never gave much thought to being a great cop either, but he was.

Another man to value his privacy, too. Kept things to himself. Thought others didn't know what was going on—like this thing with Josie. Sure, he didn't have the details, she was sick, some kind of breakdown maybe, but anyone close to Sayles who paid attention couldn't help but see the changes in him from day to day. Man was being buffeted. Graves would look over and catch him just sitting at the computer, motionless, and know he'd slipped sideways to somewhere else. Graves would look away, never said anything. You wanted privacy for yourself, you respected that of others.

Then there was this Rankin thing. Not that he was talking about it a lot, but he wasn't talking much about other cases either. And his not talking about it was kind of the point, wasn't it?

Probably had no idea that Graves knew how hard he was reaching out on this. Dolls. What was that all about? And why the secrecy, when it was their case, they were both supposed to be working it?

He'd walked past and caught the screen a couple of times, Sayles back-and-forthing with a guy Graves suspected had something to do with all this.

One thing Graves did, he paid attention.

The beer had gone half warm but he drank it anyway, in a long swallow. Moments later he felt dizzy. From one damn beer. Another of the many delights of aging.

As it alit on the rim of the fake fountain that Graves always forgot to fill with water, a grackle screeched, stabbing its curved beak to the right and left. An appeal? Indignation? Warning other birds off? Lonely?

Who the hell knew.

He set the empty bottle on the glider arm, rocked to see how far or fast he could go before the bottle fell.

Maybe he was making too much of it. The scene in the courtroom and that night in the jail cell had shaken him, no doubt about it. So maybe he wasn't thinking quite right. Still jazzed, or still beat down. Or both at the same time.

When the bottle fell, the grackle fixed him with its black eyes and squawked loudly enough to wake people three houses down. The bottle rolled and rolled, bouncing on the seams between floorboards.

# CHAPTER TWENTY-FOUR

A PIED-À-TERRE. A foothold. Something he wouldn't need for long, but for now it would do him well. When had he last had a fixed address of any sort?

What with not having to find motel rooms and be on the move, this meant one less thing to deal with. Of course, in taking the apartment he had become marginally visible. But no one—another *of course*—was looking. Or would have reason to do so.

The kid was out there playing chess by himself at the picnic table under the lemon tree. He had what Christian surmised was a fake cell phone. He'd make a move, speak into the phone, reach across to move the other player's pieces, then make his own move. Then back to the phone.

Christian picked the apartment for its proximity to a coffeehouse whose Wi-Fi he could piggyback. The ad had been on the bulletin board there, small free-standing apartment, furnished, private. One of those bottom fringes of phone numbers to tear off, but no one had.

It was half a garage behind the house, flanked on one side by bushes, on another by a sloppily mortared wall of slump block, on the third by palm trees, cholla and ocotillo. The garage half was only used for storage, the woman said. There was a good single bed with linens, a sturdy Formica-topped kitchen table, a couple of chairs, a battered black-and-white TV, a bureau with four drawers and mismatched handles, shelves on L brackets on two walls and above the toilet in the bathroom. The front window looked toward the house, rear window onto the palms and narrow alley behind.

Late afternoon now, what would be his favorite time of day if he had one, and Christian was lying on the bed, atop a plaid bedspread, counting holes in the acoustic-tile ceiling.

As a young man he'd done a single stretch in jail, in a bohunk Arkansas prison that served as warehouse for offenders of every sort, murderers to drunks and wetbrains to the seriously disturbed, from all the small towns around the state that had no place to put them, a square mile of real estate jammed to the gills with residents, equal part army barracks, high-school locker room, and killing field. This was not long after he got out of the service, when he was pretty messed up. He took his lesson from that residence: stay off the radar, fly near the treetops—always.

It was a sad excuse for decent human habitation, paint thin on the walls as though merely smeared on in passing, nothing close to plumb, cement floors crumbling away like stale crackers. Whatever contractor bid the job had pocketed a lot of money. The guards didn't look much better constructed or more durable than the walls or floor. Over the years they'd got real good at staying out of the way.

First night there, two guys held him down while another one, a squat crew-cut guy with arm muscles like Popeye's, raped him.

Staying off the radar wasn't the only thing he learned in that prison. That was also where he took to heart the virtues of planning. He bode his time, watched without looking, took notice. Where the men were, who they hung out with and when, work details, cellmates, pastimes.

First one, he caught in the auto shop. He, Boyd was his name, wasn't supposed to be there alone, but he had a deal with one of the guards. Christian put him out with a tire iron, tied him down. Then he put a funnel in his mouth and poured in a mix of battery acid and industrial solvent. Afterward, the funnel sat there cockeyed beside Boyd's head like the Tin Man's hat.

Jaco, the second, had his throat slit late one night in his bunk. The cell lock had been slipped with a thin sheet of metal. The cut was ragged, torn as much as slit. Chisels will do that. No one else in the cell saw a thing.

Christian waited for the third, the rapist himself, giving the man time to put it together, letting it build. He didn't kill that one, who went by the name Jade. He taped Jade down with duct tape as he slept, sat on his face, and took off his genitals with a loop of guitar string and two wood handles.

After that, he hadn't had any more trouble.

Late enough now that shadows lurked in corners, moving when he looked away, invisible when he looked straight on. Christian arched his back against the bed, trying to ease aching hips. Vertebrae in his neck and upper back popped in sequence, like a line of firecrackers going off.

Stay off the radar. Planning. That was what he'd learned. Things always went wrong, sure they did, but you learned to cope. To adapt, to improvise, to dodge, to divert.

But this?

Through usual channels you get the contact, the interview, the job. You compile information, reconnoiter, keep eyes and mind open. You're never able to get all the ducks in a row, but you line up as many as you can, the ones you have eyes on, the ones you suspect may be quacking about offstage. You know the location, how you're getting in, how you're getting out, your timetable. You step up—and someone else has just taken down your target.

What kind of sense does that make?

An insect—a spider carrying prey, he thought at first, then realized it was a beetle of some kind, with its wing case sprung open on one side—came from the corner about a third of the way across the ceiling and stopped there, just over the bed.

A freakish coincidence that Rankin was shot moments before Christian closed in? *Freakish*, he had no problem with. That's how life was. *Coincidence*, though . . .

That was hard to swallow.

Difficult to believe that someone else had randomly targeted Rankin. Or that chance circumstance had brought the shooter into Rankin's presence at the very moment that Christian was stepping up.

Okay. So where did that take him?

He'd been thinking that he was still invisible, that no one would come looking for him, no one would even know to look for him. But what if he was wrong?

What you always had to do was stand off, try to see it all from a different angle. It wasn't about you. He'd spent most of a lifetime doing just that.

But maybe he was wrong. Maybe it *was* about him. He was in the equation—so maybe he was an integral part of it.

He got up and walked to the window, looked out to where the kid was setting up another game, and went back to the bed.

The beetle had retreated to its corner. How long had it lived here in this room, with that crushed wing and case? What did it live on?

None of them suffered, he thought as he began to fall asleep. He could feel his mind break loose of its moorings, start to float free. None of them suffered, they all went quickly. Too much suffering in the world already. The problem comes when you start believing that the suffering, all that untold, endless suffering, has to have meaning.

A wash of images ran through his mind as he settled further into sleep. Faces, hands, his fifth-grade classroom, a sunrise he once viewed in Kentucky, a deer's body bloated and boiling with maggots at roadside, people taken over and rendered emotionless by aliens, villagers with torches climbing toward the castle, narrow corridors down which he scampered lost and late for appointments, the tunnels back in 'Nam, the ceiling above the bed in the room where he grew up.

That stained plaster ceiling gave way to this one as he drifted up out of sleep, seeing again the man's face that had turned to him from within the car outside Rankin's house, the man he'd seen back in Rankin's hospital room.

The man wasn't searching for Rankin, or keeping tabs on him. He knew where Rankin was. And from the look of things Rankin wouldn't be going anywhere.

He had been looking for Christian.

# CHAPTER TWENTY-FIVE

WHAT YOU WOUND UP REMEMBERING, what kept coming back to you, were not the whacked-out, bizarre crimes, the hatchet murders, double homicides, bunco and bank jobs, but simple things. The look in a father's eye when you told him that his son had been killed while buying a Pepsi at the AM/PM on the corner. The trumpet case that had sprung open when its owner got shot in a drive-by, and you stood there noticing the way the bell of the horn was crumpled in on itself. The half-finished castle of building blocks in an abused child's room. The suicide letter of words and phrases cut and pasted from favorite books, a crazy quilt of fonts and sizes, the books themselves put back in their places on the shelves.

Some years back he'd gone on a call to Maryvale. Caller said he was worried about his neighbor but wouldn't give any details, wondered if the police could just go by and check on him.

Man's name was Morris Hibley, and he came to the door in pajamas, blue slippers and an apron.

"If you don't mind . . . ," he said, beckoning. Sayles followed him to the kitchen, where Hibley plucked a skillet off the flame and gave the contents a quick roll clockwise. "Pulling breakfast together for my wife. Coffee should be ready"—he turned his head to glance at the coffeemaker—"if you'd like some, Officer."

Sayles accepted, and sat on a stool at the counter drinking it as Hibley went on with his cooking. He explained why he was there.

"Can't imagine why any of them would do that," Hibley said, sliding an omelet onto a plate. "Good to have neighbors watching out for you, though. Doesn't happen a lot anymore, does it?" He wiped the plate's rim with a hand towel, though it looked fine to Sayles. Alongside the omelet went sliced tomato, sauteed mushrooms, an English muffin.

Nothing was out of place. Skillet and pans square on the burners, countertop spotless, canisters for dry goods an inch apart. Even the coupons and photos on the refrigerator were straight and evenly spaced.

"I'll just run this up to Patricia and be right back," Hibley said. Minutes later he returned. The contents of the plate were untouched. Hibley made no mention of that, simply walked to the sink and scraped it all into the trash bin beneath, after which he turned and asked if Sayles would like more coffee.

Sayles thanked him and declined. "But I do need to have a quick word with your wife before I head back to the station."

"Certainly, go right up. Second door on the right. I'll just get her bath things together."

Everything, of course, was in order. The room smelled mysteriously of powders and fragrances. Pale blue drapes matched the bedspread and area rugs, as well as towels, washcloths, and wallpaper glimpsed through the open bathroom door. Darker blue candles on bureau and bedside table. Slippers like Hibley's own peeking out from beneath the bed skirt.

The bed was empty.

His wife, it turned out, had died eight months earlier. All this time, Hibley had been—in his mind—still taking care of her. Food, baths, medications. He never gave it up. They carted him off to the hospital for observation, then to court, and finally let him go, and he was still asking about her, insisting he needed to be with her. For all Sayles knew, he was over there in Maryvale fixing Patricia's breakfast right now.

# CHAPTER TWENTY-SIX

WHERE WAS HE?

He had been dreaming. Squeezing his strange body through narrow spaces, standing outside a half-open door, looking down the line of people ahead of him marching toward—something.

Then he was in a jungle, with what looked to be hundreds of monkeys all chattering at him angrily from the trees, the sour smell of his own body washing up to him in waves.

And when he woke, it was beneath a ceiling that was not his, surrounded by unfamiliar sounds, the bed's headboard scraping at the wall as he turned to look out a window showing the grayness of early dawn, then back at the ceiling across which a beetle with a crushed wing case solemnly marched.

Jimmie closed his eyes. When he reopened them, he was back in his room, but elsewhere still in his thoughts.

*His* thoughts?

No way.

Walking streets where tables filled with wares, books, CDs, watches, jewelry, glassware, had been set up outside all the shops. Germany, judging from snatches he caught of the language.

Then cobblestones, and twisting, narrow corridors between houses.

An old man wandering, head down, about the front yard.

And faces. Dozens of them, some distinct, set against walls, framed in windows, peering down from high places and out of passing cars, others floating up from the gray of sleep without surround or context.

Gray in the window, gray in his head.

He swung his feet off the bed and sat. The nail of the big toe on his right foot was broken into the quick, the others badly needed cutting. Which reminded him—the pain in his hand? He lifted it, feeling nothing at first, a dull throb slowly starting up as he put it back down on the bed.

Someone was knocking at the front door.

He made his way to the window, peered out. Two twentyish, well-dressed men in identical black pants, white shirt, and tie, carrying books close to their chests. Bibles, he assumed. Kind of early for that. Or was it?

Not according to the clock, which informed him he'd slept through till noon.

He switched on the computer, grabbed a Coke, and got back in the saddle just as the computer finished booting up. Looked at the string of headlines his search parameters had found crawling along the Web. Three, he sent to a save file. Quite a collection building up in there.

*Dog Hair May Be Clue to Cancer Cure*
*Nude Arrested at Museum*
*Suicidal Planet Spiraling Toward Star*

Deleting the rest of the headlines, he started a quick swing through his regulars, first the general sites, then the ones he cruised for plunder (flagging four items to keep watch on, buying a stone-worker's chisel inlaid with the Masonry emblem), finally setting down at the Traveler site. He hadn't been on for some time, and there were lots of fresh postings, most of them familiar territory. Interpretations of the canon, nitpicking and condemnations, cries in the wilderness. Then, near the end—it had been posted shortly before—he found:

*Things have changed here.*
*I want to come back.*
*They will not allow it.*

Someone's twisted notion of humor, right? Almost certainly. But the posting's simplicity and seeming candor, the spareness of it, took root in his imagination and wouldn't let go, left him wondering. There'd be months of back-and-forth about the posting, of course, on the site; he suspected that for a time there'd be little else.

But he had work to do.

He got supplies from the closet, brown paper, collapsed boxes, tape, bubble sheets, and spent the next hour wrapping items for shipment. He had run off labels on the computer earlier. He stacked the packages on the hall table, e-mailed FedEx for pickup tomorrow.

Now if he didn't hurry he'd be late to the hospital.

He always came in and put the book he was reading to them on the hall table, but *Candles for Chance* wasn't there. As he dressed, he tried to think what he might have done with it. Then, glancing at the clock (*he could just make it*), Jimmie picked a book at random off the shelf on his way out.

Pedalling hard, he remembered the dream of an endless line of people plodding forward, and how strange it had been to wake so disoriented, unsure where he was, unable at first to feel or control his own body. Scary, true. But kind of cool too.

A larger group than usual today, the line of parked walkers extending fully half the length of the far wall. Jimmie pulled the book out of his backpack as Mrs. Drummond in her pocket-sprung black suit was saying what a fine boy he was and that he had something special for them today as always. This should be interesting, Jimmie thought. Reading a book to them that he had not read himself, and knew nothing about. *His Monkey Wife*, by John Collier. He took a long breath and started.

*If thou be'st born to strange sights and if you don't mind picking your way through the untidy tropics of this, the globe, and this, the heart, in order to behold them, come with me into the highly colored Bargain Basement Toy Bazaar of the Upper Congo. You shall return to England very shortly.*

# CHAPTER TWENTY-SEVEN

THERE WERE PICTURES SOMEWHERE, photographs of the two of them happy together and young, or happy and healthy at least, but he couldn't find them. He hadn't been one to care for photos, never saw the point of taking them, all those people showing off endless snapshots and slides of their vacation, or their kid throwing up for the first time, or their dog. If he didn't have the memory in *here*, he'd say, and point to his head, it wasn't a memory at all, and had no value. But now he found himself at two o'clock in the morning looking for photos.

Something was fading, something was going away from him, something he couldn't put a name to and didn't want to lose.

Sayles tried to remember when he'd last slept. Two nights back, he'd finally passed out around dawn, exhausted, but you could hardly call that sleep, and what he remembered of it was like a huge room with bodies, faces, and objects of every sort crashing about everywhere, so that you could never take any of it in, never get a hold on it. He woke drenched in sweat, pulled off his clothes, and draped them across a chair back. He turned on the box fan by the couch, lay there with it blowing on him.

Feeling a familiar tug and tightness, he looked down to see an erection.

He laughed. *What a sad old fart I've turned into.*

So he had showered and made a thermos of coffee, then sat out on the porch watching lights straggle on in neighbors' houses as they eased into the new day.

Now more of the same.

Throughout those early hours and for much of the following day, pieces of his dreaming, patches, splinters, corners and edges, had come back to him. These would swim up out of nowhere, assert themselves, fall away again. In one he had been in a room lined with statues. They were stepping forward and back, turning their heads one to another, moving hands about, but they were statues. When he came into the room, they all held their hands out to him. That's all he remembered.

Last he'd seen them, years ago, the photos had been in one of those corrugated file boxes. Josie was forever into projects. She'd plan them, get everything together, be right there on the lip ready to jump, but then something else would come along and the project would never get done. In the closets were bolts of material for the drapes she'd planned to sew, along with curtain rods and hangers. A box or two of shelving bought at least eight years ago and still unassembled. Cushions for chairs snug in store wrappings, neat but ever-growing stacks of paid bills, insurance papers and correspondence fully meant to be filed away, skirts for beds and stick-on pads for furniture legs. The photos, she had sorted into envelopes according to some taxonomy all her own, time or place or subjects; they'd gone into the file box along with corner mounts, double-sided tape, scissors, a scrapbook or two.

And the box had gone . . . where?

Not in the bedroom closet, or in the hallway catch-all closet, or out in the garage where the stacks were so high and long-established that boxes on the bottom had been compressed to half their original height.

He found textbooks from the criminal science classes he'd taken at Phoenix College, stacks of old case notes, library law books he had failed to return, expired passports, X-rays and lab reports with column after column of numbers, copies of his safety records and firing range qualifications, a Bible with his name and hers in gilt letters on the inside front page, tax files and documentation going back at least twenty years, a manila envelope of programs from plays and musicals they'd attended, a lot of old clothes, a surprising quantity of new clothes still with store tags on them or in gift boxes.

And finally, under her bed, he found the photos, two fat scrapbooks full, all of them sorted chronologically and expertly affixed to the pages.

He was partway through the second scrapbook when the phone rang, Graves offering to swing by and pick him up this morning. Why the hell not? They stopped at Denny's for coffee on the way in. Sitting there watching a young couple bedecked with tattoos and piercings two booths over, Sayles told Graves about Dollman.

Typically Graves said nothing, but followed Sayles's gaze to the young couple.

"You remember that?"

"Being young?"

Graves nodded.

"And stupid?"

"And not caring that you were—that too. But I was talking about being in love."

"Isn't it the same thing?"

"Maybe. Maybe it is."

Graves waited as the server refilled their cups and again asked if there would be anything else before swinging off down the line holding the pot out in front of him like a lantern.

"You know I've never much believed in telling others how to live their lives . . . ," Graves said.

"Then now's not a good time to start, is it?"

He looked away and drank coffee. "Yeah, I guess it isn't. This stuff's nasty."

"First cup wasn't as bad."

"Always the way it is. Isn't. You know what I mean."

"Yeah, Graves, I do. Damned near every time."

"Right."

They sat without speaking as the young couple got up to leave. Sayles couldn't help but notice that the woman paid, and that the man followed her out the door, wondering what that said about the nature of their characters, of their relationship, and of the world they thought they lived in. As the couple passed by on the sidewalk outside the window, the man turned to look in at them. At some point, presumably, he'd become aware of being watched. Sayles tried to read his expression: Annoyance? Defiance? More like puzzled, he thought. What was the word? Quizzical.

"Dollman, huh?" Graves said.

"I don't have a name for him. Not that it matters much, now that he's gone to ground."

"This guy has information, looks right to have information, but he doesn't want to give it up. Yet he got in touch with you."

Sayles nodded.

"What the hell's that about?"

"I gave up trying to figure."

"So whatever he claims, we have to assume that he's directly involved."

"Chances are good."

"They're a hundred percent. And we know he has to want something. But what? He's not a suspect, there *are* no suspects—and no one even knows who he is."

"And not a joyrider," Sayles said, "or he'd have been out in the open with this from the get-go. I've been through it a hundred times. Hitchhike, minute-of-fame, self-styled Good Samaritan . . . Nothing fits."

"Something does."

The server was back. Graves's hand shot out and hovered palm down an inch above the cup. The server, Donnie according to the name tag, glanced at Sayles. Sayles looked at his watch and shook his head. "We're twenty minutes late."

"They'll start without us," Graves said, then: "Vinegar and honey. You have a snake in a hole, a kid under a table, there's two ways to go with it. You smoke him out. Or you make him think you're going to give him what he wants."

"This isn't a snake or a kid, Graves. This guy's a ghost."

"Yeah. Well, ghosts want something too—or they wouldn't still be around."

# CHAPTER TWENTY-EIGHT

THE KID WAS STILL OUT THERE, making his move on black, stopping for his phone call, making his move on white. Though now the game seemed to have become less important. He spent a lot of time between moves just talking into the phone and looking around.

Christian got a bottle of orange juice out of the half-pint refrigerator. The table limped when he set the laptop down, so he scooted the legs around till it got better. Turned the computer on and, once it powered up, found the wireless connection. It sat there quietly waiting, locked, loaded, ready.

For what?

Getting in touch with the cop, the only tangible thing he had to grab on to, had been a bust. Should he try again? Guy had probably written him off by now. Decided he was a crank or crackpot. To get his interest back—Sayles, that was his name—he'd have to give him something. An earnest, as they used to say. Something to convince him that Christian had goods, had knowledge or witness, without giving up anything about himself.

He opened a message board and scrolled down without reading. He always imagined he could hear the computer's drive whirring inside. He didn't know if it spun, if it did anything like that, if it moved at all, but he heard it. Or thought he did.

Last few weeks, he'd been having this weird sense that . . . what? That he wasn't alone? Not quite. As though someone were standing off watching or standing half a step to one side, maybe, seeing what he saw, almost a part of it. But that wasn't quite it either. A sense of presence—that was as close as he could come. The drugs, he had figured. But that sense was still with him, and the drugs weren't.

The feeling he had now was close. But different.

He turned. The kid had his nose pressed against the front window, looking in.

Christian went to the door. "Tell them I'm not here," Christian said. The kid just looked. He had brown eyes that went gold when light caught in them. "Old joke . . . You need something?"

The boy shook his head. "My name's Chris. What's yours?"

"Christian."

"Wow. We got the same name almost. Is that cool or what?"

"It's cool. You want to come in?"

"I'm not supposed to."

"And I'm thinking you were also told not to bother me."

"Yes, sir."

"Quite the moral dilemma."

"What?"

"One transgression leading inexorably to another." Christian stepped back out of the door. "Don't worry, I'll tell your mother I invited you."

"That would be lying."

"Not really—since I just did."

The boy thought about it and stepped inside.

"You like chess," Christian said.

"It's okay. One of my teachers—Mr. Stuart? He taught me. Picked out six of us, those with the highest IQs he said, and taught us. I think I'm the only one that stayed with it. You don't have much stuff, do you?"

"Only what I need."

"That's my old TV. Cool computer. Is it fast?"

"No. But then, neither am I."

"Mine's slow. Good, but slow." He took in the books stacked on the window ledge and table. "You read a lot."

"I'm guessing you do too."

"Mostly online. You can get anything you want online—newspapers from all around the world, music, books. But you know that."

"Anything you want, huh?"

"You can even order food, clothes. Never have to leave your house."

"I suppose you could."

The boy picked up the copy of *Earth Abides* atop the stack on the table and leafed through. "I read *Nicholas Nickleby* last week."

"All of it?"

"All of it."

"Online?"

"You got it."

"And never left your house."

"You're funny." The boy held up the book. "Can I borrow this?"

"Of course."

"I'll bring it back soon."

"There's no hurry."

"I read fast." He looked at the monitor screen, where the menu for a forum on animal rights hung suspended. "What do you do, Mr. Christian?"

"For a living, you mean? Not much, anymore."

"You're retired?"

"I suppose I am."

"And before?" He glanced back at the screen. "Were you a teacher? Or a biologist?"

"I was trained in the sciences. But I went another way. What about you, what are you interested in?"

The boy read the screen as they talked. "I don't know. My dad was a teacher. That was his day job, though. What he really was, was a historian. The two world wars—he knew everything about them. People wrote him from all over the world asking for information. He died three years ago."

"I'm sorry."

"Maybe I'll do something like that." The boy turned his head toward the house. "I better go. That's my mom calling. She's not calling me, she's calling the dog. But the dog never comes, so in a minute she's gonna be calling me to go look for him. His name's Rommel. He's old, and looks mean, but he's—"

"A pussycat?"

"A pussycat. That's good. That's what he is all right." At the door he turned back. "Good-bye, Mr. Christian. See you later."

"Enjoy the book."

"Yes, sir."

The boy's mother met him just outside the back door. Twice as they spoke, she glanced toward the apartment. Christian hoped the boy wouldn't get into trouble over his visit.

Christian went back to the forum, dutifully scrolled through five or six entries before realizing that he had no memory of what he had read. He drank the orange juice, warm now and fairly disgusting, and, more or less from habit, began a sweep of the sites he habitually used for communication. There were two repeated messages from people inquiring about dolls. No follow-up message on Rankin. Nothing from the cop, from Sayles.

Distractedly, with images of hard-packed dirt trails and of rooms at the edges of cities sliding through his mind, he clicked at a series of links: a piece on army dogs abandoned in the Pacific following World War II, another about a man who'd fought in both Korea and Vietnam, the review of a novel about a Desert Storm grunt's homecoming, slide shows of Revolutionary and Civil War reenactments, online stores selling authentic battle gear, memorial sites, veteran's chat rooms, history pages, Wikipedia, academic essays studded with sentences whose second clauses seemed to rip away or confound whatever meaning he had drawn from the first, further memorial sites, blogs about lost loved ones, travel pieces. Then suddenly his attention was full on the screen.

*To put things in order, this is what we all want. And here, we are on firm ground. But with the next step, the very next step, we begin to move violently apart. To some, individuals and societies alike, it is manifest that this order must be imposed, legislated, and enforced—impressed—from above. Others understand with selfsame certainty that, unless its growth is organic, unless that order comes from within, it is forever doomed.*

*I must, as you all know, return soon. My stay here has been short. I have seen so little of your world, finally, and have understood less.*

*Never forget that yours is a world of great beauty: these clouds, these trees, running water, the caress of wind. Yet so many of you do not live in it; you only visit; and choose instead to live in a world of words, of theories.*

*You are trapped, prisoners in your language, hostage to your insistence upon understanding.*

*Theories rule, and will destroy, your world.*

Hours later, well into the night, when little of the world remained around him save the sound of an occasional passing car and the spill of moonlight over half the table, Christian got out of bed, turned on the computer, and tried to find the posting again. But try as he might, he couldn't recover it, couldn't reconstruct the steps that took him there. As he searched, moonlight moved across the surface of the table in a slow tide, touched his hands, and moved on.

# CHAPTER TWENTY-NINE

"SO LET'S SEE if we can call up the spirits."

Graves rolled the chair in close, hands on the keyboard. He sat there rocking two inches forward, two inches back, wheels squeaking. Man couldn't just sit in a chair to save himself. Always had to be scooting, rocking, keeping time. Not from nervousness or tamped-in energy, though. This was something else.

In quick succession, too fast for Sayles to follow (he spotted Google and Dogpile as they zipped past), Graves entered *dolls* on a stream of search engines, then, appending a series of qualifiers here and there, moved the search ("Let things perk a while") to the left half of a split screen. He went on keying—John Rankin, the *Arizona Republic* for the days following the shooting, *New Times*, Good Sam and other central hospitals, fire department and city records, half a dozen addresses—in what seemed free association. Screen after screen came up, bloomed with prompt boxes or site jumps, and dropped to the bottom bar. Good soldiers.

Sayles watched Gonzalez move with his coffee mug down the aisle between desks. *Barge* was the word that came to mind, not barge in the sense of rushing, but in that of a river barge pushing its dogged way upstream. Gonzalez had been shot last year during a routine traffic stop, then while in the hospital and almost recovered, got hit by a stroke. Came back from that, too, but to permanent desk duty. Did okay on the whole, but you could see in his face, in the pitch of his body, the concentration required even for simple tasks. The mug was a gift from his wife, customized with his shield number, and it was never more than two-thirds full. He held it well out in front, balancing himself with the other arm, eyes on the mug as though it were a carpenter's level.

Sayles heard the snap of Sanders biting into an apple at the next desk. When had the chair wheels stopped squeaking?

Graves leaned back. "This is interesting."

Unable to make much of what he saw on the screen, Sayles shook his head.

"I put in Rankin's address, sent out a crawler for activity in the vicinity."

"And?"

"A recent nine-one-one call just up the street from Rankin's place, man unconscious in car. Paramedics responded with on-site treatment and transported. Probably just a coincidence, but . . ." Graves reached for the phone. "Let's ask."

Sayles noted with interest that Graves dialed the number from memory. And to a direct line, no getting passed along. A few moments of back-and-forth banter—someone he knew, obviously—then Graves asked his question.

Silence.

Graves swung the mouthpiece up. "Cooking."

Then the phone went back, he listened, he said how much he appreciated it.

"It just got better," he said as he hung up. "Caucasian male, late fifties to mid-sixties. Seriously ill, treated in ER, moves to a room—and he rabbits. No trace of him."

"The hospital has to have—"

"He's carrying a driver's license with his picture. Shows his name as Gerald Hopkins. A case worker at the hospital tried to follow through when he went AMA. The license—"

"Was a fake."

"And no other ID. A nurse in ER remembers that he said his name was Christian."

"Another dead end. So we don't know anything."

"We know one thing."

Sayles waited.

"We know he's dying," Graves said.

Dark night of the soul. There it was, looking in at him.

Sayles stood at the window. He'd stepped down the room to get away from the glare of computer screens and desk lamps. They were there, but off to the side, behind, distant and apart.

It was 2:48 A.M.

It was 2:48 A.M and Sayles was thinking how, despite white nights, a redoubling case load, and everything else that was going on, he never felt strung out anymore. Normal—that's what would feel weird.

Stretched out flat on his back on the floor by their desks taking what he insisted upon calling a power nap, Graves was snoring. From the break room came the smell of burned coffee and the sound of the unwatched TV playing what seemed to be the same commercial over and over, something about the music we all love, before giving way to a program on the social behavior of cats and dogs.

They'd been to the hospital, then to every convenience store, gas station, coffeehouse, bar, and hole-in-the-wall nearby. Adding old-fashioned legwork to the enpixeled shadowboxing that, if you believed TV shows, solved all the crimes these days.

Sayles was thinking about one where the agents, detectives, whatever they were, rarely stepped out from behind handheld computers, oversize screens, and smart boards. They'd talk, the resident geek would hit the keyboard, after a while a couple of them would wander outside for a brief car chase or gun battle, then they'd be back in the game room. Need information? Rub the lamp. Driver's license, passport, school and employment records, bank statements . . . all a keystroke away. Need photos? Tap into the security cameras at the pawnshop across the street.

How many viewers, he wondered, paused to think what this said about rights to privacy? Or stopped to wonder how easily these agents, detectives, whatever they were (fictional, of course), might be able to track you cradle to grave, follow you through damn near every hour of your day and days.

Not exactly the way it went, here in the real world. For all his reaching and all his volleys, Graves hadn't got jackshit on Dollman.

Out there in the night, twin spotlights lashed the sky. Some store's grand opening, or a bar hustling customers, or a sale at one of the stretch of car lots along Camelback. And someone forgot to shut down the lights.

*When dogs play,* a level-voiced announcer was saying on TV, *they employ actions common to such activities as actual fighting, or mating—biting, mounting, and so on. It becomes important for them to signal their intent, to broadcast what they want.*

*The social order requires that the dogs agree to play and not to eat one another or fight or try to mate.*

Despite himself, Sayles broke into laughter.

So, zilch on the Internet, and the legwork hadn't done them any better. One half-assed lead from the backroom guy at a flower shop. Guy's arms were about the diameter of a baseball bat, dark brown and shrunken-looking, as if they'd been half-cooked. The tattoos that once covered them had faded away, remnants of their color serving only to add to the skin's unhealthy look.

He remembered, he said, because he'd been sitting outside on a long-delayed break, this humongous, hurry-up order for carnations and sunflowers, some poncy school thing out Mesa way. He was about to light his cigarette when he saw this soldier coming down the street. That's what he said: soldier. "Man looked like shit, you know? And I'm thinking, Whoa . . . seen *this* before. Fuck flashbacks, they're bullshit—propaganda, you with me?—but for a minute there I thought I was back in country."

The timing was right, and when Graves asked what direction the soldier came from, the man pointed north, where at that moment a medevac helicopter was settling onto the hospital roof. But that was it. The man had nothing more to tell them, and neither did anyone else.

Luckily, Lieutenant Byerlein wasn't hands-on, content to be left alone to tidy up paperwork and study for the law courses he was forever taking. They told him they'd be pursuing leads on another case, might run into overtime. They wouldn't put in for it, but the presumption would cover their absence from the squad, use of department resources, working off shift, and, they hoped, whatever else came up.

*Whatever else* had not, in their minds, included something like forty hours straight without much by way of break or food. Sayles's eyes wouldn't focus for more than minutes at a time. He could feel his body blurring, the border between it and the world around him breaking down, dissolving.

When he turned back from the window, Graves had resumed his seat by the computer. His finger hit the keys, a single sharp peck. His eyes went from what was on the screen to Sayles.

"Yo," he said. "If you told me, I don't remember, how'd you get onto the doll thing in the first place?"

"Came from a CI, when I was trolling. Didn't think anything of it till I got the message."

"From Dollman."

"Right."

"And it said 'I sell dolls'?"

Sayles nodded.

"Interesting." Graves's chair was still. "You think he advertises?"

Sayles walked over behind him.

Graves pointed to a line of text on the screen. "This is from *Lock & Load*, basically a newsletter for mercenaries. Private security, bodyguard work, like that. And this, this, this"—he looked up at Sayles—"are off the Web, message boards at three different sites."

*Please confirm shipment of the doll ordered Feb 10.*

*I am an avid collector, and am interested in purchasing one of your exceptional dolls.*

*Would like to obtain another doll from you. Please contact me ASAP.*

*Please inform me whether you have dolls still for sale.*

"The first one's from a couple years back." Graves did something that changed the screen. The other messages dimmed, leaving the last two highlighted. "These were sent through the same IP, roughly the same time of day, a week apart. Hang on . . . Here's a third, just posted."

*I am looking for a special doll for a special friend.*

Graves dragged it across the screen to line up with the other two, stared a moment, then looked up. "They're talking about something other than dolls."

"One definitely gets that feeling."

"All worded similarly, could easily be to the same person."

"Form and placement suggesting they don't know the seller. Lot of walls between."

"So, it's not dolls, what is he selling, what are they trying to buy?" Graves pointed to the two highlighted lines. "Whoever posted these, if it's the same person, he seems . . . eager?"

"Doesn't help us much. We don't even know who they are."

Graves hit more keys. "Maybe it does. They're looking, same as we are. And it's not them we're looking for." Screens bloomed, dropped to the bottom. "These are ads, right? Break them down, that's what they are. So . . ."

His chair went back into motion, two inches forward, two inches back.

"So we place our own ads."

# CHAPTER THIRTY

WHEN HE TOOK THE CHILI to Mrs. Flores, she'd insisted on dishing it into one of her own bowls and sending his bowl back home with him. Jimmie stood by the kitchen door waiting. Her friend Felix was sitting at the kitchen table with a glass and a bottle of liquor. Jimmie had never seen that except in movies. Felix asked how his hand was, how he was doing.

Chili was about the only thing his father ever cooked. He'd make gallons of it in this big cast-iron pot and they'd live for a week off that and boxes of crackers, which the old man always called saltines. Jimmie still liked the chili but he didn't fix it much, and he always wound up throwing a lot of it away.

He wondered if Felix and Mrs. Flores would really eat it.

Chopping onions and peppers and all had been a little scary at first, and he figured it to be that way for a while. Early this morning he'd been awakened by his hand hurting. Then when he held it up, he realized that it wasn't hurting at all; he'd been dreaming that it hurt. He didn't remember much of the rest of the dream. He was in a room somewhere, blond furniture squared against the walls, pictures above, flowers, mountains, bodies of water—what he imagined a motel room might look like.

And lizards. There were lizards in his dream. Now he remembered that.

They were everywhere: on the ceiling above him, silhouetted in the window against light from outside, peering over the edge of picture frames. All of them perfectly still.

The other day, after he read to the old folks at the hospital and was packing up to go, Mrs. Drummond approached him to say they were having a holiday get-together for everyone and she hoped that Jimmie and his parents would come. It would be so *nice*, she said, pausing on the word, to get the chance to meet them, and to tell them how much Jimmie's work there was appreciated.

Duck and run time.

He had to wonder if he was growing careless, complacent, taking too much for granted. And all at once he had remembered his father saying "That's how they get you, boy. Nice home, cushy job, comforts." It was the flip side of his old man's other habitual diatribe: "They keep you under their thumb, boy. Always pushing, always bearing down, till you can't move, can't breathe."

Leaving the hospital, he had passed a sign in the hallway, yellow and black, *Danger* at the top, *Hazardous Materials Area* and *Authorized Personnel Only* to the right beside a circle enclosing a slashed-out human figure. It occurred to him then that much of what parents tell children is hazardous material and should come with such warning labels.

This was one of those days when nothing felt right. Dreams. Lizards. His bedclothes looked like something that had been used to wrap leftover food. Even the house seemed vaguely unfamiliar when he came in from running the chili down to Mrs. Flores. He supposed that making the chili had been his try to get things back the way they were. And he wondered how much of the world's activity was aimed toward trying to get things back the way they were—or back the way people imagined things were.

The kitchen, of course, was a mess. And that was something he could fix.

Half an hour later there's a rack full of clean dishes, the hot water heater out in the utility room's thumping as it recharges, there are pools of water on counter and floor, and he doesn't remember any of it.

Kind of scary. Where had he been?

Then, slowly, it came back.

He was in a yard, then a house. Blankets folded and stacked on the couch, pillow with a pink pillowcase on top. Shelves packed with display dishes and knickknacks, paintings on the wall, long curtains at the windows. He walks through an arched doorway into the kitchen. Coffee makings, pans, empty cans in the trash, lunch meat and old eggs in the refrigerator. A table with stacks of paper, a computer, pens, a notebook. He is going through it all. Slowly going through it all.

He watches as his hands pull a legal pad toward him and write, *Please contact me. This is for you alone. I sell dolls.*

# CHAPTER THIRTY-ONE

HE BLINKED, trying to make sense of what he saw, what he thought he saw.

Dark shapes at the window, against the light. Like pods or small fish. Commas. Leaves. The f-holes of violins and guitars. Then, as his eyes moved from there to the wall and ceiling, more of them. Six, eight, a dozen. And one, he realizes now, on his hand. He lifts the hand slowly, moves it closer to his face, and the two of them watch one another. Its skin is cool and dry, tissue-thin, amazingly soft. With each breath its sides flare. He sees the tiny, intricate cage of ribs.

What a beautiful thing it is.

And so many of them, so many of these small beautiful things that fill the world around us, unnoticed, unacknowledged, unseen.

He remembered the kid saying "Hope you like lizards."

Well, yeah.

Popping the top off his last orange juice, he did the same with the computer, gulped as it booted up. Just past dawn, six or a little after, maybe? So that was the most sleep he'd had in a single stretch for a while. Odd that he hadn't needed desperately to pee when he woke up. He checked his feet and ankles. A little swelling, not a lot more than normal. Hand shaking some, he'd noticed that earlier with the lizard, but if there was discoloration, jaundice, he couldn't see it.

The lizards had begun retreating.

Because he was up and moving around? Or because they had duties to attend to?

Geckos. Amazing little creatures. Feet an absolute marvel of nature's trial-and-error engineering. That many in plain sight, there'd be nests, in the walls, or right outside. A single parthenogenetic female could populate an island. New ones were tiny—tadpole-size. They moved like mercury, tails often left behind with confused attackers as they sped away.

And now, a confused attacker was what he himself had become.

All those years, he never much pondered what he did. What it meant, what he left behind as he walked away. He'd known early on, from navigating the situation at home and from his reading, that he was a problem solver. That's what life was, a string of problems to be solved. And what he did for *his* living, from inception through planning to execution—from start, to had to, to happen—that was no different.

But this time the *had to* hadn't happened.

Problem.

And he still hadn't peed. God help him if his kidneys were shutting down. He turned to look out the window where the morning built slowly, filling itself with the sound of cars and birds and garage doors and shouting children.

*God help him.*

How had that got in his head? Not a metaphor he owned—for

all his belief that we understand our world and guide our lives by metaphors, that we can scarcely think without them.

What of animals, then? Did they think abstractly? When animals played—was that abstract thought? Obviously, from the paw twitches and changes in breathing as they slept, they dreamed. The smells surrounding it were a dog's metaphors.

Did the gecko sit on the ceiling remembering where it was born, the warmth, other bodies? Did it think how it lost its tail, wonder how long before the new one grew, even as it waited for the fly to land within striking distance?

—And exactly where, he thought, looking back at his hands to resurface, did all *that* come from?

He reached again to probe at his ankle and decided to let it be.

Back in country he'd served as de facto medic. Everyone came to him with their complaints and questions, wanting advice: rash and athlete's foot, sores, shrunken dicks, swollen dicks, constipation, bleeding gums, hangnails, torn muscles, night sweats. Not much he or anyone else could do about most of it.

Just like this.

For so long, time held no meaning for him, one day like another, years little more than a jumble of passing seasons. Now time was solidifying around him.

You grow up hearing these things people are saying over and over all around you, *He's a good man*, *It's in her blood*, *I should have known*, *Live and let live*, and you never give them much thought. They're just *there*, like rocks or walls or sky. Then one day you stop and think, What the hell's that mean? The one that always got him was *Everything happens for a reason*.

Sure it does.

He shouldered his attention back to the computer, cruising the sites that, bone-weary and distracted, he'd given up on last night, after the kid left. The two older messages inquiring about dolls were there, of course.

And interestingly enough, crowded up against those at both sites, this one:

> Special doll for sale.
> The one you've been looking for.

# CHAPTER THIRTY-TWO

THEY'D BEEN OUTSIDE Rankin's house going on five hours now. Situation like this, you used up conversation topics pretty fast, not that they hadn't already, all these years they'd worked together. So they were sitting there silently. Graves was thinking about Sayles's wife, and about an old case.

He got dispatched to a house out in Mesa where the kid, fourteen or so, had been refusing to eat, claiming it was to purify himself or somesuch thing. He was so weak he couldn't get out of bed, looked like a praying mantis with a human face. The kid's sister, three years younger, had dialed 911. Uniforms responded, saw what was going on, and called back in for a detective. Over the following days Graves had watched parents, doctors, and courts fight over whether the kid could and should be force-fed. They were still fighting when, at the hospital, the kid picked up an infection that took him out.

Graves unscrewed the cap off a bottle of Arrowhead water, took a slug. Offered it and put the cap back. "We don't have a clue what we're looking for."

"Nope."

It wasn't much of a connection, but for the time being it was what they had. Maybe the guy the paramedics had picked up out here, the one who went AWOL at the hospital, was involved, maybe he was the one they were looking for. Dollman. Maybe he'd return. Maybe he was already here.

Maybe their pockets had big holes in them.

All told, it was a quiet neighborhood. Mainly Anglo, so not much life on the street, houses closed off, yards empty. Just people dodging from house to car and back, the odd few out mowing or whacking weeds. Guy five houses over working in his garage with the door cranked open, classic rock seeping from a cheap boom box.

A kid went by on his bike, backpack laced onto the handlebars. An old bike, looked like one Graves himself might have had as a kid, not one of these spiffy new things with a dozen gears and skinny-ass tires. In truly great shape, though. Kid probably ought to be in school, Graves thought; then thought that it wasn't any of his business.

Half hour or so later, without saying anything, he and Sayles watched an older man come around the southeast corner and walk slowly down the sidewalk on Rankin's side. He was wearing a light summer suit, or a sportcoat and slacks, and limping. Going past the house, no pause, no change, he continued on around the long curve and out of sight.

Graves turned on the radio low. Sayles glanced his way but didn't say anything.

"Give it another hour and pack it in?"

"Okay by me," Sayles said.

Guy on the newscast was going on about this holiday tragedy, how some family's father got laid off with a wife in the hospital and three young kids at home. Yeah, right, Graves thought. Tragedy. Tragedy was about fatal flaws, about bottoming out emotionally, physically, spiritually. Tragedy was a twelve-year-old killed by gangs on his way to school, the eighty-year-old judge who'd sat thousands of cases and now couldn't remember where or who he was. You had air space to fill, it got filled—like gas filling whatever container it's put into. And knowing how insignificant most of it was, you cranked it, shifted to hyperbole, smeared lipstick on the pig. This guy? Pitiable, yes. But a couple towns over from tragic.

"It would help if we had some idea what we're looking for," Graves said.

"And how often does that happen, that we know what we're looking for?" Sayles reached over and turned off the radio. "But in this case it's quite conceivable that we're looking for a Honda"—he nodded toward the tan car pulling abreast of them—"that went by at 9:36 and again at 13:42."

Single occupant, male, brown hair. Sayles was scribbling the plate number on the pad clipped to the dash. "Be a good time to have a cam—"

Graves held up his cell phone. "Got it."

The plate went with a rental from National—not the Honda.

"Now there's a surprise," Sayles said.

The car itself matched four recently reported missing, including one from long-term parking at Sky Harbor.

"Okay, two surprises."

Sayles was peering out at the long, almost empty room. He had a way of doing that, Graves thought, like he'd suddenly surfaced from somewhere else. "Where the hell is everyone?"

"Holiday. Everyone the bosses figure we can do without is home."

"Makes you wonder, doesn't it?"

"About what?"

"The bosses, to start with. Then about how much work actually gets done around here."

"Guess it could . . . We want to put the plate and vehicle out there?"

"Yes."

Graves picked up the phone.

"No."

He put it back.

"This guy took the car from long-term parking, not a glitch, not a wobble. Grabbed plates somewhere else and swapped them. What's that tell us?"

"He gets things done."

"Right. He's the guy we're looking for. Has to be."

"But you don't want a flag up?"

"He knows how things work, he probably knows a lot about what we do, too. Right now the car's all we have. Let's not give him a push to ditch it."

"So, what? We take up full-time residence outside Rankin's house, wait for this guy to cruise by?"

"Maybe."

"Okay. What's plan B, then?"

"Hell if I know."

As they talked, Graves had been rummaging in his computer. Now his fingers paused on the keyboard.

"Here's another surprise."

"Okay."

"A posting just like what we put up, advertising a doll for sale. 'One of the rarest, maybe one of a kind.'"

"Our man?"

"It doesn't feel like it, does it?"

"If it's not him, not Dollman, then who is it?"

"Someone looking for him? Same as we are."

He felt it the minute he walked in.

All the drive home this thing had been turning over and over in his head. *Same as we are*, Graves had said. Maybe so, maybe not—which described this whole mess, start to finish. Rankin was alive, but someone, for some reason, was dogging him. Maybe the shooter, maybe not. They had the car, the Honda, that the someone was in—and which could disappear at any moment. And then there was Dollman, who had seen it—seen something—go down. Was he part of it? Maybe so, maybe not. And these ads. Did they mean anything? Or were they just another dead end?

Round and round. Over and over. He was still thinking about it when he opened the front door.

Then he wasn't.

Because he felt the change then.

There was nothing different about the room. His neat stack of blankets and pillows remained on the couch. Room tidied up, but the carpet unswept for some time now, a haze of dust on shelves and knickknacks. That familiar musty, long-unaired smell.

She was in the kitchen, sitting at the table. The nurse he'd met at the hospice stood off a bit, near the refrigerator, and nodded. He stopped in the doorway.

"You're keeping late hours, Dale."

"As always."

"You remember Judy Zelazny. She's off duty, but when I told her my thoughts, she insisted upon bringing me." Her hands were in her lap. She had lost more weight. The blue bandanna on her head matched the blouse she was wearing. "The old year is almost gone, Dale. I wanted to come and thank you for it. And to wish you a happier new one."

"I could have come—"

"I needed it to be here, in our world, Dale. Not there."

"I understand."

"You always did."

She stood, hands on the table, then straightened and walked toward him. He could see that Ms. Zelazny's impulse was to step up and help, but she pulled back. Josie came to him and he held her. He felt the curve of her ribs, like a boat's hull, felt her heart beating just beneath the skin. There was so little left of her.

"I miss you," he said. And feeling her tremble, helped her back to the chair.

"I'll wait in the other room," Ms. Zelazny said.

So much came back to him, so many memories in a flood—he could see the same in her eyes—and yet, so little to say. He sat watching her chest heave as she caught her breath.

"I have to get back soon," she said. "It's good to see you smile."

"A few more minutes . . ."

"There are always a few more minutes, Dale."

Not always, he would think later as he watched Ms. Zelazny's van pull away. But for now there was small talk: others at the hospice, how was Graves doing, the crazy neighbor who the whole time they'd been in the house had kept building a fence and tearing it down, the bar that just reopened under new management for the fourth time this year up the street, the young woman in a long dress and plain dark clothes she watched go by each day outside her window.

Then she was gone. He sat on the couch, not really thinking, not really remembering, just *there*, floating, strangely free. He heard cars pass, someone blowing wildly into a trumpet or trombone, a moth buzzing at the window, what sounded like thunder far off, blood pounding in his ears. When he looked up, it was morning and Graves stood by the open front door.

# CHAPTER THIRTY-THREE

THESE TWO WERE ABOUT as subtle as a preacher's fart during a moment of silence for the dearly departed.

Keep walking.

No question it was a stakeout, and almost certainly what's his name, Sayles. And his Sancho Panza. Question was, why. The shooting had gone cold by now, the cops had to have better things to do, Rankin was alive, and there didn't seem to be anyone around to care. So why were these two still on the train? They didn't know that Rankin had other eyes on him, or about the new doll postings—couldn't. Or could they?

So he kept walking, carrying his plastic bag—like he'd run up the street for a pint of ice cream or milk and was heading back home.

Heading home. He was, of course. Just like in all those gruesome, mournful Protestant hymns.

But not right now.

He stuffed the plastic bag in a mailbox as he passed. With the cops hibernating in their car, he was out of here, didn't need protective coloration anymore. He couldn't even remember what was in the bag, something he'd picked up at a Circle K or AM/PM.

You always think your life is heading for something: some grand turning point, the moral decision that will define you forever after, an outcome. Medical school. Happiness. A profession. Family. Saving the free world.

A block or so up from Rankin's, as he'd come out of the alleyway where trash bins and abandoned furniture stood sentry, a bicycle had passed on the street. Nice old bike, knapsack threaded through the handlebars. Kind of bike, back in his day it might have had plastic streamers coming off the handlebar grips. The rider, early teens maybe, looked to be deep in thought, and Christian wondered now if the boy thought *he* was heading for something.

The tan Honda had come by twice, once a couple of hours back, give or take, while he was sitting on a low wall up the street with a newspaper he'd snagged, again not too long after he spotted the stakeout, just before he ditched the plastic bag.

That night he had one of those dreams where he knew he was dreaming, where sometimes it seemed he was the central character, it was happening to him, and other times like he was just watching from a distance, a mute witness. He was standing in an apartment that looked familiar but continued on forever, on into shadow past the couch, table, chairs, and rugs he knew. At first he was speaking to someone, but then the someone became an image, a photograph or an uncompleted painting, or a mirror, but it wasn't himself he saw in it.

You thought you would change the world, the image's voice said, no trace of threat or challenge, simply conversational.

Maybe . . . once, he responded. Then: Don't we all, when we're young?

We lose the dream.

Maybe we have to, to go on. Or maybe we only misplace it, as we do so much else.

Is that why we are all so sad?

Are we? Sad? How can we be, with life so full around us, with so very much in the world to engage us?

But always the bad ending.

Is the ending what matters?

He woke in sheets damp with his sweat. Without pain, though, and strangely at peace. Needing desperately to pee. Pitch-black outside and in. Had there been another power outage? He stumbled over the chair on his way to the window, looked out, and still could see nothing. It was then he realized he was blind.

# CHAPTER THIRTY-FOUR

HE HAD *HIS MONKEY WIFE* in his backpack, the backpack lashed to the handlebars, and he was wondering where everyone was. This wasn't a way he usually came. Nor did he know why he took the route today. Got to the end of his street, to the edge of his neighborhood, then turned on impulse into Fern. Fern was a long, long street that snaked through three different apartment complexes. The street was unnaturally wide but, because the apartment lots were dense with trees, didn't look or feel wide. It looked narrow and dark, and it felt claustrophobic.

Having run the chute, he spilled out into *this* neighborhood, something with Gables in the name, he saw on one of those little signs they add to the regular street signs. Coral Gables, Green Gables, Clark Gables, something like that. Like this was some special, defined place, apart from the jumble.

He was thinking about the people he read to, wondering what their lives were like. Dark and narrow, like the street he just left? Or bright, empty, and unlived-in, like this Whatever Gables?

One of the few signs of life was a couple of men sitting in a car at curbside. They both faced forward, the driver slouched down, the other sitting up straight—maybe looking for something? Neither was talking.

What did those people at the center think about? What kind of expectations, what kind of memories, did they have? He was pretty sure they hadn't imagined their lives coming down to what they were.

Last night he had foundered in a dream, the world gone pitch-black around him, him feeling his way, one hand high, one low, along a wall. No memory or idea where the wall might lead, but it was solid, it was what he had to hold on to, it was *there*. He sensed (maybe, he thought later, maybe it was the sound of his own breathing reflected back at him) that he was coming to something, an end, a corner, a doorway. Then he had come fully awake and realized he was in his bedroom, pressed up against the inside wall, paralyzed.

The dream stayed with him, an afterimage superimposed on everything he saw and touched around him, making it all seem vaguely unreal or distant. The dream was beside him through breakfast and the clean-up, there through a much-needed shower as he examined his finger (healing, but still no sensation in it), there as he sat at his computer, there for the run through his regular sites. Only when he'd settled to work did it fade.

He had three e-mails inquiring after shipments. This was not good—and not like him at all. Those items should have gone out days ago. He responded, apologizing, pleading a sudden upswing in business and promising immediate shipment or, if that proved unsatisfactory, a full refund.

Two of the items, he had boxed and ready to go. He printed a label for the third and left it in the printer tray to remind himself, then e-mailed for pickup.

Both a collector in Michigan and what appeared to be a small specialty museum in Ohio had e-mailed about the antique optics set he had posted, eleven lenses used maybe a hundred years ago to test vision, each lens in its own leather case, the set itself housed in a beautifully crafted teakwood box.

Another requested additional photos of the child's pink porcelain tea service.

A man to whom he had sold a small banjo with the painting of a blackface minstrel on its head and, later, a "Rastus" ventriloquist dummy, e-mailed to ask if by chance he had come across any new examples of plantation art.

The rest of the e-mails were straightforward and easily dealt with. After that, and after he wrote a couple of checks, yearly insurance on the house, and a "donation" payment to the free clinic (*This is not a bill*), he was done.

He clicked back over to his favorite sites and backed through the subsequent commentary—was it real? a hoax? what did it say, and what did it *really* say?—to the latest entry from Traveler. He read the posting over and over.

> *My stay here has been short. I have seen so little of your world, finally, and have understood less.*
>
> *Never forget that yours is a world of great beauty: these clouds, these trees, running water, the caress of wind. Yet so many of you do not live in it; you only visit; and choose instead to live in a world of words, of theories.*

That night, thinking of Traveler's posting, he remembered how it had felt riding his bike that afternoon, how he had been all alone moving through the world, he remembered the sun's warmth, the wind on his skin, and he remembered the faces of the people he read for, as though he had brought them something precious, something extraordinary, instead of just a story from an old secondhand book.

Jimmie walked through the kitchen into the garage. Here was a story, too, one he had pieced together. Apparently, after his mother left, his father had gone out, bought heavy storage boxes from a moving company, and packed up everything he deemed hers. The boxes sat as they had sat for years, perfectly stacked, perfectly aligned, against the garage's rear wall, a solid block two deep, four wide, and taller than he was, each box carefully labeled.

Jimmie went out to the porch, to the glider whose frame had rusted through last year so that now one side dragged on the floor. He heard, from another porch, another house, someone shouting angrily. The moon was bright. It hung in the sky out over the Superstitions and seemed not to move at all, as though it had all the time in the world.

# CHAPTER THIRTY-FIVE

"AND HOW DO YOU feel about that?" Graves looked out to where a fat man and a car needing a tire change were fighting it out at curbside. "Listen to me, I sound like some damn social worker."

Sayles laughed. "Yeah. You have to talk about it," he said. "Get it out there. Don't hold in."

"Learn to let go."

Sayles glanced over as the light changed. "Man, I feel so much better now."

Graves was about to tell him enjoy it while you can, the bill's coming, but Sayles went on.

"How I feel, is that she was saying good-bye."

Graves made no response. They were pulling into an area that had once been central Phoenix but was now a two-mile stretch of crumbling churches, front-room tax preparers, the odd chiropractor, and blasted houses, some of them caved in or partially burned out.

"Interesting choice for a meeting place," Sayles said.

"The mall?"

"Fight your way past the skateboarders covering the parking

lot, you get to the old folks inside. Median age is what, sixteen? Fit right in."

"There's a Denny's, round the back."

"That thing's still there? That used to be the regular stop out this way when I first went on the force."

"Like most of us, it's not what it used to be, but it is still there."

A scatter of bedraggled cars occupied the parking lot. Most of the mall's business these days came from the neighborhood, or got bussed in. Besides, it was early in the day. Close to a dozen Hispanic males stood by one of the entrances, hoping for day work.

"You think there's anything to this?"

"Has to be." Graves looked out at the hopeful workers. "Those guys have families, you think?"

"Most of them. Here *and* back home."

Graves shook his head. "That sucks."

"Yep."

"Well . . . Like I told you, I went in early, thinking I'd at least do a run-through and update on our files—you know, the cases we've been ignoring? I'd just got started when the first e-mail came in."

"And it said—"

"Dolls. I hit reply and sent a question mark. When he came back with Officer Sayles?, I said yes. He wanted to know if you were still interested in someone connected with a shooting at the Brell building. The message was garbled, but readable. No way I thought it was really him, not at first, and there was all kinds of weirdness—misspellings, run-ons. But he had the correct address for the shooting."

"And he asked for help."

"Not in so many words, but that's what came across. Said he had been contacted by the person he thought responsible for the incident."

"Still guarding his words."

"Right. And that he'd set up a meet he was unable to make. Just let it hang there. So after a minute of staring at the cursor blinking, I said maybe I, meaning we, could help with that, make the meet for him. That's when he sent through the details. I asked how we could contact him, but he was gone. Dead air."

Sayles pulled in at the Denny's. Two other cars in the lot, those plus a pickup with sideboards made of scrap lumber, filled with yard tools and palm cuttings.

"We been chasing this guy how long, and he comes and finds us?"

"Hey, it works for deer hunters."

"Graves, you're a city boy, what the hell do you know about hunting?"

"I read. I listen to people."

"Sure you do. So why us? The thought that we're getting set up for something cross your mind?"

"More than once . . . Maybe we're all he has."

"All he has for what? We don't know who he is, what he wants, how he fits in."

"Maybe we're about to find out."

They were out of the car, walking to the door. "You're full to the top with maybes today."

"Think positive."

Despite the span of windows, what with the posters and three-inch-high letters of painted-on specials obscuring them, not to mention the dinginess of those windows or the lack of internal lighting, walking in was like entering a bar, some zone of perpetual evening. A young man in overalls sat at the counter forking in eggs with one hand, texting with the other. Four other singles sat around the room. The waitress was leaning into the order window talking with the cook.

Graves and Sayles took a table near, but not too near, the door. The waitress brought water, not something you saw a lot anymore, and menus. Sayles opened a menu. Its once glossy surface was thick with ancient smears and spillings.

"Samples," Graves said. "You want breakfast?"

"I'm going to check out the bathroom and the back. Order for me."

"What do you want?"

"Doesn't matter, it all tastes pretty much the same."

"Good point."

Graves watched the waitress make a swing through the front, refilling everyone's coffee, on her way to their table. She set the carafe down at the edge, took out her pad, and told him the specials. He ordered two.

"Large juice is only twenty cents extra."

"Why not? Two tall oranges. Thanks."

She smiled, then ducked her head. Sensitive about the crooked teeth, he figured. Been doing that her whole life.

Two new diners came in while Sayles was away, a twentyish couple in what looked to be self-consciously thrift-store clothes. Another left, climbing into a Pinto with cardboard taped over a rear window and red plastic film over both tail lights. The food arrived shortly after Sayles. Minutes later a new patron entered.

"Hunter's vest," Graves said.

"Got it."

One of those guys who looked young till you took a closer look, wearing what Graves's father to his dying day had called dungarees—jeans to the rest of us—and, under the vest, a blue dress shirt, sleeves rolled to his elbows. Unlined face, save around the mouth and eyes. Light brown hair still full, not thinning, but dry-looking, dull.

He walked by the counter, glancing this way and that, then around the corner into the back area.

"What do you think?" Graves said.

The man came out from the back and sat at the counter. The waitress stepped in, brought him a coffee, asked if there was anything else.

"I think he knows who he's looking for, by sight."

"Our man, you think?"

"Could be. And maybe you could stop jamming those eggs in your mouth long enough to go check the parking lot."

Graves went out, circled the building, returned.

"It's around back, almost out of sight."

"Tan Honda?"

"You got it."

Together they stood, leaving the food half eaten, and stepped toward the counter. The waitress's head turned. She said something, and the cook came out a side door, leaned against the wall watching.

The man didn't look around, but he knew they were there. You could see it in his shoulders.

"You have a doll for sale, I believe," Sayles said.

They'd stopped a yard away. Now the guy turned. His eyes went from Sayles to Graves back to Sayles.

"You're not Christian."

"Your friend couldn't make it."

"My friend . . . right. So he sent you."

"That's about it."

"And who would you be?"

Graves took out his case, held up the badge. The cook nodded and went back into the kitchen.

"Cops," the man said. "He sent cops. That's pretty funny."

Graves and Sayles took the stools on either side.

"Guess that means you don't want to buy the doll, huh?"

"Tell you the truth," Sayles said, "we're not even sure what a doll has to do with it."

"Interesting," the man said.

Sayles smiled. That was one of Graves's favorite expressions.

"That you're looking for me, I mean, and don't know why."

"We suspect that it has something to do with a shooting that occurred some time back. At the Brell building?"

"Right now," Graves added, "we need to see some ID."

The man took out his wallet and set it on the counter.

"Thank you, Mr."—Graves flipped it open—"Barnes." Then, to Sayles: "Carroll Barnes. Local. No credit cards, couple thousand cash, give or take."

"You're not going to tell us we need a warrant for that?" Sayles asked.

"Figure you learned that in cop school."

"Are you armed, Mr. Barnes?"

He shook his head, then asked, "How is Christian? But wait, you came in here not knowing who you were looking for. Do you at least know *him*? And how he's doing?"

"Something else we don't know, I'm afraid," Sayles said.

Graves added, "We haven't met him."

"Makes this quite the reunion, doesn't it?"

"Let's get back to the shooting," Sayles said. "Tell me about John Rankin."

The waitress advanced apologetically behind the counter. "Are you going to finish your breakfasts, or should I clear the table?"

Make room for all the waiting customers, Graves thought. "Go ahead. We could use some fresh coffee, though."

She nodded, brought prefilled cups for both of them, then went about seeing to the remains. The cook was keeping an eye on them while doing his best to appear not to.

"I don't know John Rankin," Carroll Barnes said.

"Christian, then."

"Interesting. I don't know John Rankin, but you don't seem to know much at all."

Sayles was silent, signaling with his eyes for Graves to stay quiet too. It was all about negative space—something a lot of interviewers never learned. Space has to be there, to get filled.

"Do you even know what he does for a living?"

Sayles shook his head, waited.

"He's a hit man, a contract killer. Has been for forty years. Probably longer."

"Interesting," Graves said, and the three of them exchanged glances.

"Can I assume that I'm under arrest?"

Again Sayles said nothing.

"Or," Barnes went on, "is that something else you don't know?" What might have been a laugh, or just the man clearing his throat, sounded. "I suppose it was only a matter of time."

# CHAPTER THIRTY-SIX

BY MORNING, sight had partially returned. The day was out there, just beyond reach, shot with shadows and restless, ever-moving bright spots like silver buttons, everything blurred at center and edges, as though the world were gradually excusing itself from existence.

Which, he supposed, was exactly what it was doing.

He had managed to feel and fumble his way to the back door of the house to ask Mrs. Guinner if it would be possible for Chris to come out for a minute or two, he could use a little help.

"Are you okay?"

"Slightly under the weather, I think," he said. "Nothing contagious."

"Christopher is upstairs getting ready for school. I'll send him right out."

He thanked her and did his level best to walk back across the patio as though nothing were amiss. He could feel her eyes on him, sense the questions behind them.

He'd scarcely got back inside and into his chair when Chris showed up. Heard the boy's feet dragging across the cement, through the grass. Then the boy was at the door and, suddenly, right in front of him.

"I brought you something," and an elongated shape moved toward him. He reached out.

A book. Slim, paperback. Cover heavily creased, page corners so ruffled and burred that they must look like tiny carnations.

"It's one of my favorites. Kinda goofy in parts, but pretty cool."

He felt the boy's eyes on him, like the mother's, but he didn't sense unspoken questions behind them, only a waiting, an eagerness to take in as much of the world as would offer itself.

"Thank you."

"Mom told me you wanted something?"

So together they had rearranged the room, dragging table and chair over to the window where the extra light helped a little, moving the lamp in close. He had the boy boot up the computer for him, figured he might be able to take it from there. When they were done and Chris said he had to get to school, nevertheless he hung back. Not wanting to presume or intrude, Christian thought, but seeming to understand more than made sense given Christian's beggarly explanation. Where did someone his age get that kind of intuition, that kind of sensitivity?

"I could come back after school, if you want. If that's all right."

"That would be great. Thank you. For the help, and for the book."

Shortly thereafter he was sitting with his face three inches from the computer screen, shutting his eyes and opening them again and again, trying to resolve ramshackle lines and shapes into words, into meaning.

*Special doll for sale.*
*The one you've been looking for.*

He'd answered that posting last night. And now there was a response. Leaning still closer, he was able to make out the letters—reconstruct them really, piece by piece. Like a child learning to read. And fumbling his fingers around the keys with the font kicked ridiculously high, he was able to cobble together his own response.

The timing sucked, for sure. But this was it, the hole, the rabbit, and it wasn't likely to turn up again. No way he could make it to the meet he'd just set up, of course. Only one thing to do.

So this is what it's come to, he thought, more than half amused. This of all things. Going to the police for help.

# CHAPTER THIRTY-SEVEN

EVERYTHING WAS DARK. He lifted his hand, knew it was in front of his face but couldn't see it, however close it came. A blur, nothing more—and even that, he could be imagining. Imagination clicked in hard as you lay unseeing. Sounds came, and you worked to affix substance to them: the refrigerator cycling on, the front door settling in its frame with the change in temperature, a tree limb scratching at the roof. And as you listened, more and more sounds made their way to you, an unsuspected world of them, another, alternate world.

Somewhere (the fire station?) a chain rang against its flagpole.

A helicopter hovered, swung away and was back, out over I-17.

Getting to his feet, he took three steps and stumbled against, what? A chair, a table edge? The thought came that he'd have to move the furniture, put it back against the walls. As though this was the way it was going to be forever now.

But it was not his thought. And not him (he thought, waking) moving through that place where everything was dark.

# CHAPTER THIRTY-EIGHT

SURPRISED? Not at all. How could I be? As I said, the way things went down, I knew it was just a matter of time. Funny how things never go the way you think they will, how they always get so tangled up. Our lives aren't a hell of a lot more than that, are they? A bunch of tangles.

I didn't shoot anyone, though. Hell, turns out I didn't really do much of anything. Ran around a lot, tripped over my own feet and everybody else's. When here I thought I had it all worked out. My old man used to say I was dumb as a rock, far back as I can remember. Maybe he was right after all, that ass-wipe.

Guy you're chasing, he's a ghost, a shadow. No one knows who he is, no one's ever seen him. That lived to tell about it, anyways. You go looking, and look hard enough in the right direction, a bunch of names pop up. Doc Watkins, Stu Carter, John Brown, Bill Gaunt. And that's about the whole of it. Names, smoke. Fumes.

But you know what this guy does for a living, so you go at it backward.

I was twelve years old. Came home from school one day, least I was supposed to have been in school, and there's a police car in the driveway. Not the first time, mind you, but this time it was different. Chief Winfrey was waiting to tell me my old man was dead. He'd had his throat cut a few hours back, when he was in the bath with a bottle and the radio tuned to the country station.

You know, I've always wondered what miserable cheatin'-and-drinkin' song he was listening to when he died.

I'd never seen Chief Winfrey look uncomfortable before, but he did. Kept turning his hat in his hand, round and round, and glancing at the window. "I had the boys take your mother over to the hospital," he told me. "She's okay, just real upset."

He always said, right there at the first and any time it came up later, that something wasn't right about the whole thing. Killings back there and then, they happened in the street, or in backyards when kinfolk got into it, or up in the woods. No one walked into a man's house in broad daylight and slit his throat while he was in his bathtub and then just walked out and vanished.

Like I say, I was twelve, what the fuck did I know, I could barely get my pants on straight. I knew my life had changed, I wasn't that dumb, but it took a long time before I realized how *much* it had changed.

Then one day—I'm out of college by then, earning my keep, as my mom would say—I'm in a bar after work and the guy next to me's a retired cop. He gets to talking about this one case he could never get over, never forget. Wife came home and found her husband sitting in his favorite armchair—thing was all butt-sprung and worn through, the cop said, but every time she'd try to throw it out, *he*'d throw a fit. Anyway, he was sitting there with his head back like he was catching a nap, but when she walked up close she saw his eyes. That was what she saw first, the cop said. His eyes. Then, a little farther along, she saw how his neck was all swollen and bruised where he'd been choked to death, with a braided wire of some kind.

Thing was, he, this cop, could never find any reason for it. Man had no one set against him, far as could be found. His trucking business was in trouble, but with the economy back then, so were better than half the businesses in town. And no way was it a crime of passion. It was cold, calculated, done by someone with a lot of strength who knew exactly what he was doing.

Someone brought in for the job, the cop said, that's what I always thought. Never found hide or hair of him.

How would you even go about looking for someone like that, I asked him. And over the next few beers he lays it out for me, how you look for cognates. That's what he called them, cognates. Carryovers, derivatives. How people so often use names like those they've used before, same initials, same number of syllables. How the way they eat, the way they dress, doesn't change that much. How people tend to stay with the same kind of work, whatever name and background they've shifted into place.

Find the work, he said, you can find the money. And once you have that . . .

I paid the tab for both of us, which by that time was big enough that I knew I'd be hurting till the next payday, and I carried what he'd said out of there and back to my apartment, one of those godawful places with mirrors and shiny metal everywhere you look.

Not long after that, and early in the game, I got into computers. Tech stuff at first, then designing them, software finally. The future came to me one day in a chat room as I watched some guys grousing about the census, that they'd only answered how many people were living at the residence and mailed it back in, because that's all the government needed to know—or saying they'd just thrown the damn thing away. And I'm sitting there thinking, You fuckers slide your MasterCard at Kmart or run your Exxon card, you're giving away a hell of a lot more than that. Nowadays, I'm thinking, damn near anything you get involved in is floating around somewhere out there. You buy something, there's a record. You borrow a book from the library, there's a record. Your kid's baseball team loses, that's out there too. Cyberspace. It's like this huge field that goes on forever, and there's footprints everywhere, going every which way.

Getting involved—that was the key. No one just sits alone in a room. However much off the grid you stay, sooner or later you have to get involved with *something*.

The site I was browsing that day belonged to a bunch of libertarian types, people who spent their time discussing inexhaustibly their privacy and rights and God-given freedom.

Like their right to bear arms. Pry it from my cold dead hands, etc. So okay, I figured, guns is one place this'll take me. Lots of options, a man could spend his life bouncing like a pinball from one site to another. And once you're there, it's a hop, skip and a jump to homeschooling, spyware in our telephones, killer vaccinations, survivalists, secret societies, war enacters, and mercenaries. So for the next few months I had a guided tour, with myself as guide, of every organization, every ragtag club, every cockeyed assembly and midnight gathering that stood three steps to one side or another of the mainstream culture.

Took a long time, but I found my way. I went on the notion that Chief Winfrey was right, and whatever the reason for it—I never did know that, and never will—someone had been brought in. And that ex-cop back at the bar, the one who got me started on this—same thing. I still didn't know who I was looking for, or where to look, really.

Just like you.

But I knew what the man did. And to do that, he had to be hooked in somewhere, somehow, to this social underbelly I'd been getting to know. Lot of these sites had sections with people trying to maybe sell a gun or trade it for a hunting bow, or areas where they'd offer to barter services for goods, or sell collectibles. Good places to start, I thought. So I started running ads and responding to them. Spent hours getting them worded right, vague but not too vague, you know? Not like you can come right out and put *I need someone killed*, right?

You have to say it without saying it.

Most of the responses I got—well, most of them were just crap, but the ones that had a germ to them, a certain smell, those I followed up on—they were like that too, trying to say something without seeming to say much of anything. You'd get a headache from squinting, trying to read between the lines. Then you log in three, four responses and it gets *really* hard. Like you're both waiting for the other one to blink, you know? That's the point that most of them just fall away. So you keep plugging, poking about in there to see what's what.

Till finally, and let me tell you, it took me a while, I had my A list.

Obviously an audition, some kind of trial run—show me what you got—wasn't in the picture.

It was after work, this neighborhood place half a block off Camelback where I'd go afternoons, watch people, drink overpriced coffee. Looked up from my laptop and saw this guy heading out the door with one of those cardboard trays for carry-out coffee, but only one cup in it. How he's dressed, look on his face, the way he goes through the door sideways, that single cup, it's . . . I don't know, not sad or anything, just . . . blank? I follow him and like I thought, he's going back to work. I see where he works, an accounting firm, and the name, and I think no wonder the guy's not beaming with pleasure at life.

There are two vehicles left in the parking lot out back, a shiny black pickup with locked cover, a recent Hyundai. No way this guy drives a truck, so I get the license number of the Hyundai. Only sign of life I see's on the second floor, down near the corner, someone standing close to the window with a carry cup, looking out.

Next day I called up Quality Accounting, explained how I'd met one of their staff at a function and he'd given me his card but I'd misplaced it, and gave them a description. "At a function?" Ms. How-May-I-Direct-You said, as though I'd told her we ran into one another on Mars. So now I had his name, where he worked, car and license number. Another late-afternoon visit to the Brell building and a short ride later, I also had a couple of photos and where he lived.

Ducks in a row.

Good to go.

All five on my A list got the information. Four, I sent money; the last, I never heard any more from. So there I am, don't know any of the four of them any more than they know me, who they are, what they plan. So now I'm a sentinel. Hanging. Watching. From the car, from benches or low walls, from a restaurant half a block up the street. Place probably has a name, but *Home Cooking* and *Daily Specials* is what you notice, painted on the front window, big yellow letters. I'd sit in the front, watch my building through those letters. Trying to suss out who worked there, who belonged. Who didn't.

Drank a lot of coffee sitting there, and the whole thing happened on one of my bathroom breaks. Came back out to all this commotion across the street.

You know what happened, the guy that actually got in, the one that went for it, he bungled the job. And the others, they're not around anymore, after that—if they ever were. Knew what happened and to stay away, maybe. Took the money and ran.

I had a suspicion, though. Just because I wasn't seeing them didn't mean they weren't there. Once it's quiet again across the street, I slide over and talk to some folks sitting outside, get some skinny, and find out where the ambulance was headed.

I think I saw him at the hospital. At the time . . . Well, no way I could be sure, just had that feeling, you know? But then, when I spotted him at the house, I knew. Had to be him. Watching the house just like me, nondescript car, nothing to draw attention to himself. Next thing I know, he's passed out there in the car, close to dead for all I can tell. I make the call, firemen come—then before I can blink twice, he's gone again, not a trace, not a footstep.

Christian.

So that's all I know, all I have to hold on to. Still, in the long run, I did better than you guys, didn't I?

Revenge? Yeah, right . . . How many things can you guys get wrong? Not that you'd have any way of knowing. How badly off base you are, I mean.

My father was a monster. I was a kid, I thought my mother's skin was naturally purple. I'd hear things at night no child should ever hear. Then go down in the morning and there she'd be, fixing breakfast with her eyes swollen so bad she could barely see, using the one arm that was still working, sort of. Revenge? Hell, I was looking for the man to *thank* him. For saving my mother's life. And for making my own possible.

# CHAPTER THIRTY-NINE

"YOU GOING IN, OR WHAT?"

"I have a choice?"

"Probably just as soon shoot yourself in the head."

"Come right down to it, that's pretty much what it feels like."

"I'll wait out here."

"You don't have to."

"Sure I do."

The moon made a long shadow of him on the drive as Sayles got out. A middle-aged woman with a decided limp, nurse or nurse's aide, waited inside and opened the front door for him. They went down a lime green hallway he didn't remember from the time before. The walls had waist-high tread marks where stretchers had bumped and slid along them. Three workers sat around a long table at the nurse's station. All looked up. Soft music played on a yellow plastic radio at one end of the table. To him it sounded like *hush-hush-hush*.

Sayles figured he'd spent his life not caring about the things most people did, not reacting the way people thought he should, not saying the things people always say without once looking behind the words, and now he just sat quietly by the bed. The woman went away, came back some time later to bring him a portable phone, the doctor calling from his home to explain what had happened and offer his condolences. We know you're in pain right now, the doctor said.

Nothing like the pain she was in, Sayles thought. And the pain, he figured, is always there, something we carry with us all our lives, just dormant until something wakes it up, reminds us it's there.

He thanked the doctor and sat there a while longer. When he climbed back in the car, Graves didn't say anything. They pulled out, drove by Good Samaritan, tire stores, a Goodwill, a Mexican seafood restaurant, Glad Gals Lounge. Sayles thought about the yellow radio back at the hospice.

He was still thinking when Graves shut off the engine. They'd been sitting in front of his house a couple of minutes.

"Don't want to go in, you can crash with me," Graves said.

"Thanks. I appreciate all this, man."

"It's nothing."

A 747 floated low overhead, gliding into Sky Harbor. Somewhere back in the oleanders behind the house, doves called.

"You ever think of yourself as a hero?" Graves said.

"You kidding?"

"Some of us, that's what gets us on the job to start with. Do some good, stand up for what's right. So you don't?"

"Think of myself as a hero? No way."

"Maybe other people do."

"I doubt it."

"But you never know, do you? Maybe other people look at you, they've been wondering why they go on when it's so damn hard and getting harder all the time, and it keeps them on the job. Maybe they don't know how to say that, even to themselves."

"And maybe they go chasing some ghost, not because they think it's worth doing, but because it's important to a friend? You think I didn't know that?"

Graves shook his head. "People." He reached across and opened the passenger door. "Get out of here, Sayles, get some rest. See you in the morning."

When he was young, he would get up early just to see the sunrise, to be a part of the morning. Sit out on the porch or in the yard under a tree, watch light gather, feel the new day come alive around him.

He can't see much of anything now, but light and dark and shadow are left, so he knows it's coming on to morning, and he feels the warmth on his skin here by the window. Curious how he is not asleep yet all these dreamlike images run through his head. Rooms, hallways, streets. Always going somewhere else, or preparing to. Always a mix of anticipation and apprehension. And animals—every sort of animal. Kangaroos at the door when he answers it. Rhino snouts poking in at the window. Slithery things in the bathtub. A silver fox sitting at the table with him.

He remembers the cruelty of children back home, who would catch garfish, prop their mouths open with sticks, and put them back in the water to rise and dive and rise again and finally drown. They'd say they were making submarines.

He remembers Black Dog, sick and covered with ants.

He remembers sitting on the porch in the rain, reading his medical books, finding his way around bodies. Life and disease, life and its end, so intertwined.

He remembers, with an emotion he cannot put a name to, his first kill.

He remembers the art teacher he had in college, who kept saying You have to look! You have to see! They'd be there, the model sitting on a chair, and this teacher, Miss Formby, walking around, watching what they were doing. Not just the model, she'd say. Look at what's around the model. What's between her and the chair. What's above and below her. The silence that enfolds her. Draw that.

At the time he'd had precious little idea what she was going on about. Now he wonders if it's only in the surround—what's around us, the silence and charged air, the places, other people, the sunlight of a new day—that we exist at all.

The TV is on behind him, back in the room, volume turned low. A program about the Impressionists, which, he realizes, is what brought him to remembering Miss Formby. Something else starting up now. He hears the calls of birds.

Chattering and flapping and cawing, the birds woke him. A yellow cat was after them, moving slowly, body lowered, along the wall by the birds' favorite tree. He banged on the window and the cat poured off the wall, to the other side. He'd hit the window frame with the side of his hand, but now he felt pain, the throb of it, in his damaged finger.

Stupid.

Tatters and tendrils of dreams curled about his head. Trees so thick that you couldn't see the sky, so green that the faces of the men walking next to him were green too. A child—there one moment, then gone as it lifted its head. An office, everything pale green and blue, walls hung with framed posters of the circulatory system, bones and joints of the feet, flexion exercises. A man whose eyes go empty as he looks down, watches.

Strange.

Pulling on his T-shirt, he wondered about the stains. Not too bad, you'd almost think they were part of the seascape or the bear or whatever was on the shirt long ago before it faded. But time to do laundry, definitely. He'd been letting way too many things slide.

Like having his hand looked at, when he wasn't sure it was healing right. Mrs. Flores said she'd take him to the free clinic, or Felix would, no problem. He'd go over later today, find out what time was good for them.

Right now, though, he had business to take care of, and should get started. He grabbed a bottle of juice and booted up the computer but soon found himself wandering the halls of cyberspace instead of working.

*Where Is Traveler?*

*He came to us, changed our lives, and now he is gone.*

Followed by the usual spate of conciliatory posts: Traveler will always be with us. We are all Traveler. Everything happens for a reason. Traveler *will* return.

Jimmie thought how, in the initial post, the loss shone out so purely, so strongly, and how the rest, instead of responding to that loss, tried to pretend it wasn't there, to disguise it, dismantle it, deny it.

People leave us, he thought, they leave us and they're gone. Family, youth, places we've lived, what was once important to us. All our lives are a going-away. Maybe we have to pretend that we're going *toward* something, hang the image there in the air ahead. A better, more equitable world. Life everlasting in a place that looks like Scottsdale only better. A desert oasis with seventeen virgins. Because we can't bear the thought that this is all there is. All there was.

He thought back to his dreams before the birds woke him this morning. He'd been sitting on a porch listening to rain come down. He couldn't see the rain, couldn't see anything really, but that didn't seem strange, and he could feel the warmth blowing in through the screens, smell the dampness, the green, life. And there too, in the dream, he could hear the call of birds.

# CHAPTER FORTY

SAYLES GOT OFF THE ELEVATOR. Lights were low, even in the halls. It was like being underwater, suspended between day and night. Standing still, you could sense, just out of hearing, the thrum of hundreds of engines: heaters, cooling machines, ventilators, centrifuges, cookstoves, recording devices, phones, intercoms, pumps.

Graves was waiting for him by the elevator.

"Come on back, we're good."

They passed through automatic doors into an ICU with beds arranged in a fan around a central nurse's station. Each room in the unit was a different color, with paintings to match. The rooms were carpeted as well. Thinking what went on here, Sayles found himself wondering how often they had to tear the carpet out and replace it.

"I had an alert out to all area hospitals. One of the few things we knew about him is that the guy's sick, right?"

Their man was in a pale blue room toward the back. Four IVs hung at bedside, three clear, one bright yellow. Sayles took in the room, the monitors. Heart rate high—artificially sustained, or trying to compensate for a blood pressure of 90/55? Not good either way.

"Kid found him and called it in. He was living in an apartment out back of their house. Boy gave his name as Christian. They found my alert and the old ER records about the same time. So here we are."

"It's him?"

"Has to be."

The man looked well groomed even at three in the morning in this ghostly light wearing a hospital gown—hair pushed casually to one side, features full and symmetrical, nails clipped in careful rounds. Sayles peered closely at the skin on his arms, the whites of his eyes. Mid-sixties, he was figuring. Right around five-ten, one-eighty. Tight build.

"He had a directive in his wallet, signed and notarized, requesting no resuscitation, no extraordinary measures. That was the only document on him. They're making him comfortable, as they say."

"Yeah, they do say that."

"Sorry, Sayles, I—"

"No problem. And thanks for the call."

"Almost didn't, considering."

"Good that you did."

A nurse, male, Hispanic, came in to spot-check vitals, nodding to them. He glanced up at the TV with its newsman or commentator mouthing away silently, and turned it off with one hand as he adjusted the drip on an IV with the other. Nodded again as he left.

They stood quietly looking down at the man, his breathing so shallow it barely showed.

"Hard to imagine what his life must have been like," Graves said.

"Hard to imagine what anyone's life is like, from the outside."

"Yeah, we see that every day, don't we." Graves looked up at the empty screen, then at the window, also dark. "How many men you think he killed?"

"I don't think it matters anymore."

"Yeah, I get that, too." After a minute he added: "You think he knows we're here?"

"Anybody's guess," Sayles said. "Staff always tells you, Talk to them, it'll make a difference, they'll know."

Sayles bent close to the bed. In that moment he thought of all the things he might say—about understanding, about what mattered now, about it being okay to let go, about finding rest. But what he whispered, lips inches from the man's ear, was something much simpler: *You're not alone*.

He'd been sitting by the window, feeling the sun on his skin, his mind roaming. Floating. The jungle was there, and many rooms in many cities, many faces. Animals.

He remembers that much, then nothing.

It is dark again now, he can tell that, so time has passed. How much, he has no idea.

Two men stand near him talking. Another was there, then gone.

He wonders if he could move, should he try. Or speak. Surprised that he feels nothing of what one might reasonably expect: fear, grief, anticipation. Loss, yes, how could he not feel that. But most of all what he feels is a strange peace coming over him, filling him.

It is almost, he thinks, over.

One of the men bends to speak to him.

And now he remembers. A program about dogs in Moscow, swelling up in the room behind him—that's what had been on as he sat there in the morning sunlight. Adapting to changing conditions, dogs had learned to use Moscow's complicated subway system. Many were strays; others rode in daily from suburban locations to take advantage of the bounties at the city's center.

When capitalism came to Russia, the old industrial complexes were shoehorned out of the city to make room for shopping centers, restaurants, and apartment blocks. Dogs, who had long used these as shelters, moved with them—and now commuted.

In the city, though color-blind, they had learned to cross the street with traffic lights. They were so much loved, so much a part of the city, that when one of the strays was stabbed to death, officials erected a bronze statue to it. Others fed the dogs, built winter shelters for them, shared their seats on the metro.

The dogs, scientists say, have an exact sense of time. They know their destination, their regular stops.

Moscow's dogs work, another authority said, for peaceful coexistence. On the metro they are affable, even docile. They rarely beg for food, which is given them anyway. They cross streets with the other pedestrians. They are doing what we all do: their level best to adapt to a world forever changing around us.

He remembered.

He had turned his head to the television, and for a moment, just for that single moment, his vision returned. That was the last thing he saw, the last thing he would see. A dog standing on the platform waiting for its train.

. . .

Jimmie turned his head through moonlight to look again at the clock. A little after four in the morning. No birds now. Soon, though. Been in this bed so long, and so long awake, that he felt the grit on the sheets against his skin. And when he threw back the sheet, the sweetish sour odor of his body drifted up to him.

Had he remembered bills this month? And for that matter, had he had any money coming in recently? When was the last time he'd gone hunting for bargains? Man, he used to love doing that. Things were changing. He started to understand a little how his parents would lose track, how they couldn't keep up.

He'd always paid such close attention. He had to get back to doing that.

He had gone to sleep almost at once, then woke an hour later feeling . . . empty? He was lying in exactly the same position as when he first lay down, left side, knees drawn up, face turned into the pillow. He hadn't moved.

For a moment upon waking he thought he heard music far off, then decided it was nothing more than random sounds around him, wind, water in pipes, the old house settling, that his mind turned to something more.

He lifted his hand, the finger cleaned and rebandaged before he went to bed, into the light. Sirens started up close by, at the firehouse three streets over, he assumed, then abruptly stopped.

Maybe he'd get up after all, fix some food. Whack another finger.

Or check out his usual sites. But that prospect didn't do much more for him right now than looking for stuff to buy and sell. It felt to him as though something had changed forever, and he didn't even know what the something was. And that, the pretense of it, made him laugh, at the very moment the sirens started up again. He listened to them squall down the street out of hearing, off to whatever fire, accident, emergency waited. How frail our hold is, he thought. And what a small wind it takes to blow it all apart.

He understood then why he'd awakened, what the emptiness was.

He had been dreamless.

The dreams that had come to fill his nights, the dreams that had become so much a part of his life—they were not there. And he felt their absence with the same uncomprehending despair a man feels at the loss of arms, legs, the ability to stand and walk. An ache, an emptiness.

Jimmie looks to the window where a moth flutters at the pane, across which car lights periodically sweep. With no premeditation and no true realization of what he is doing, Jimmie parts his lips and says quietly: "*Are you there?*" He says it again, and waits.

Later, with dawn advancing tile by tile across the floor, he'll get up and go to his computer. He will sit there a long time, listening to the sound of the day starting up around him, before turning the computer on. It will be many long months, a winter and a spring, before he dreams again.